The Greek Constellations - Taurus

The Greek Constellations - Taurus

Stephan De Jonghe

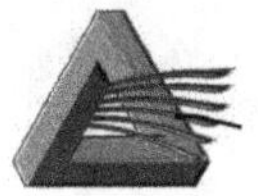

Contents

Copyright

Publisher
Stephan De Jonghe Publishing,
Hillarys, Perth, Western Australia, Australia 6025

Printer and distributor
Ingram Content Group
1 Ingram Blvd.
La Vergne, Tennessee USA 37086

Cover

In the footsteps of Homer and Hesiod.

From Astronomy to Mythology

How the constellations came to be named by the Greek God's.

Stephan J De Jonghe

Novella Four

The constellation Taurus

The legend of the Jupiter's Moon Europa and the constellations of the Taurus the White Bull, Canis Major or Laelaps the dog, Canis Minor or the Teumessian Fox, and Draco or the Dragon.

The dedication

The dedication.

To say that my darling wife is the love of my life
is an understatement.

Deb is my best friend, soul mate, confidant, and life partner.

Among so many other things, we also share a love of books, and we have
a massive library on display in our home of books that we want to read.

Our topics include action, comedy, romance, science fiction, crime,
thrillers, and adventure.
We also have an impressive non-fiction collection.

My endeavours as an author represent a passion that
burns powerfully for me. I am driven to write.

I have many stories to tell and writing them and publishing them is my
way of contributing to other people's library's.

Writing involves many hours of research and then sitting in solitude,
slowly assembling the words that details a journey into a readable story.
One that was only previously an idea.

This takes a lot of patience and persistence.
After the story is put down, the process of editing begins.

Few non-writers understand that this stage can take as much five times longer than it takes to write the actual first draft.

My Deb gives me the support that I need to execute my writing passion. She not only supports my writing, but also enjoys reading the stories.

Her assistance with proof reading, feed-back on content, and editing, is invaluable.
Especially after I have become blind to my own errors.
She understands how important it is to me and to you, the reader, to get it right.

I dedicate these books to my wife as my thanks to her for her ongoing support, and for her contributions to the finished publications.

We are a team.

We both hope that you enjoy this series of books, and we look forward to your feedback.

Stephan and Deb De Jonghe

Special thanks

My special thanks go to Janey Emery – Renowned Australian artist, for giving me permission to use her art for the covers for my Greek Constellation series of books.

"I hope you enjoy her art and the story within these pages."
Stephan De Jonghe - Author

Janey's Story   - Born   in Narrogin,   Western   Australia, Janey Emery's interest in art began as early as 2 years of age and led to art becoming the central element in Janey's Childhood. Excelling in art throughout her school years Janey devoted herself to the art course provided by Balcatta Senior High school, where her passion for art only intensified.

Janey has been painting fulltime since 1991 and has attained a high degree of respect in the art world from peers and art lovers alike. Janey has won numerous distinguished artistic awards for her work and has sold many paintings throughout Australia and overseas. Janey Emery is achieving the recognition her distinctive artistic talents deserve.

Janey is Self-Taught in All Mediums with the exception of leisure courses undertaken in oil and water colours.

"Art has always played a part of who I am. From early childhood to now there has been a need for me to express myself through drawing and painting. I find peace in my craft, and I hope I bring that to my paintings."

"To me, my Art is like breathing. Painting is my life."
Janey Emery - Artist
https://www.janeyemery.art/

Authors note

Author's note: Many thousands of years ago, the origin of the constellation Taurus was one of the many stories imagined by ancient travelers and sailors. This story is based on Ancient Greek mythology and is about why Zeus created the Bull constellation in honour of his love for an African Princess named Europa. "Taurus" is the Latin name for "bull". This story is set in a time before Zeus's formal union with Hera.

Many of these stories owe some of their earlier history to the Phoenicians, Babylonians, and Mycenaean's, and were initially used to help ancient travelers remember star patterns as a night-time navigational tool. Over time, these fascinating stories were greatly embellished on how the constellations came to be formed. The ancient Greeks called these constellations the "Katasterismoi" meaning, "the placing of the stars." They gave names and told stories about forty-eight out of the eighty-eight constellations that are recognised by the International Astronomical Union.

These mythologies were embellished as they were countlessly re-told with tales of gods encountering wild creatures, fighting fierce battles, and of course having lots of sex. After all, these men were away from home for lengthy periods of time. They shared these stories to entertain urban dwellers that they encountered, and from there the stories became legends, and for many people they became their religion.

A Greek poet and storyteller named Homer, was the first person to document these stories and he is most famous for the "Iliad" and the "Odyssey" which he composed some 2,800 years ago. Whilst very little is known about Homer, he is regarded by many as the founder of modern literature. His two main works were the first literary works to be taught formally to students. Interestingly, there are thirty-three film adaptations of the Odyssey, proving his works are still relevant to modern audiences.

Later, a poet named Hesiod, significantly contributed to Greek mythology and followed on from Homer's work. Together they are attributed with establishing ancient Greek religious customs, formal astronomy, the development of structured learning, documenting events, early economics, commercial farming, and time keeping.

The word "zodiac" originated from the Greek words "Zodiakos kuklos," meaning "circle of little animals". It was not until 50BCE that the first classical zodiac depicting the twelve astrological star signs in their current order was first depicted. It is known as the "Dendera zodiac."

During the 2nd century CE, a Greco-Roman astrologer and astronomer named Claudius Ptolemy worked on his documented Tetrabiblos into what is regarded as western astrology's primary source document and remains largely in use today. Also of note is that astronomers have named a crater on the Luna surface, and another on the surface of the planet Mars Ptolemaeus, in honour of Ptolemy and his contribution to astronomy.

The connection between Greek names and Roman names for the same deities came from their translation from one language to the other. In ancient Greek, Zeus is pronounced Dias. In Latin that became Djous Pater (Sky father) or Luppiter. In English this became Jupiter. Many names evolved in this way.

As an author, my goal is to turn what is known of the mythology into an enjoyable story for today's reader.

Stephan J De Jonghe

Chronology

Chronology – Yet another note from the author, Stephan De Jonghe

My "from astronomy to mythology" series of novellas posed some difficulties in terms of writing the stories into a logical chronology. Until the Iliad, and the Odessey, no one had ever written any of the tales of titan's forming the world, or their ultimate defeat by the gods who eventually resided in Mount Olympus. These stories were imagined piecemeal, embellished, refined, and retold over a thousand-year period. Unlike history, which did happen on a linear timeline and can be plotted, the timeline used in fictional stories were not relevant, and by their very nature at the whim of the storyteller. Over the millennia, re-tellers of the stories frequently added details, and characters that were often inconsistent with the other stories. No one knew and no one cared, as they were mostly just for entertainment.

For the more serious devotees, these stories were the basis for a religion, and many aspects of the stories were used to focus worshippers' attention, and they were therefore treated by many at the time as historical facts. They focused their attention on those gods and goddesses that were consistent with their beliefs and values.

The best example that I can use to demonstrate the challenge of chronology, is referencing a main character known as Pandora. As she is the first human woman, she features in her own story, but she was created by Hephaestus, the son of Zeus and Hera, and it happened when Zeus and Hera were already married. But Zeus met and fell in love with Europa, a human woman, who was alive before he married

Hera, and before he had a son to ask to make the first woman. Challenging!

As an author with a particular attention to detail, (at least I believe I do), the chronology of Greek mythological events became increasing important to me as the list of novellas planned for this series grew to thirteen.

I have therefore prepared a simple chronology (that may or may not be consistent with other writers of this genre) to assist readers in sorting out the sequence of events that occur in the stories that I am sharing with you. (Spoiler alert!)

I now believe that Greek Mythology Chronology should be a legitimised field of study all on its own. (Perhaps it already is?)

<u>The novella.</u>	<u>The details of the event.</u>
Pisces	Gaia forms the earth, oceans and skies. She is the earth mother.
Pisces	Gaia gives birth to Uranus.
Pisces	Cronus is born and defeats Uranus when he is released from confinement.
Pisces	Aphrodite is born.
Capricorn	Pricus is the father of the sea-goats.
Pisces	Cronus is crowned king and marries Rea. Zeus is one of their six children.
Centaurus	Cronus mates with Philyra. Chiron is born.
Pandora	Prometheus creates a race of human men - It is known as the golden age.
Pisces	Zeus defeats Cronus and Zeus is crowned King of the Gods.
Pisces	Zeus marries Metis, Athena is born, but Metis dies.

Pandora	Prometheus creates a second race of human men - It is known as the silver age.
Pandora	Prometheus creates a third race of human men - It is known as the bronze age.
Pisces	Zeus marries but then quickly divorces Themis.
Pandora	Prometheus creates a fourth race of human men - It is known as the iron age.
Sagittarius	Crotus invents the bow and arrow.
Pisces	Zeus marries Hera. Ares, Eileithyia, Hephaestus, and Hebe are born.
Pisces	Aphrodite arrives at Mount Olympus and marries Hephaestus.
Pandora	Hephaestus creates Pandora as the first human woman.
Taurus	Zeus meets Europa.
Scorpio	Zeus mates with Leto and Apollo and Artemis are born.
Scorpio	Poseidon mates with Euryale and Orion is born.
Scorpio	Atalanta is recused as an infant and she now runs with Artemis
Aries	Zeus creates a cloud nymph named Nephele.
Aries	Poseidon mates with Theophane and Chrysomallos is born.
Aries	Nephele marries Athamas and Helle and Phrixus are born.
Aries	Chrysomallos rescues Helle and Phrixus.
Ophiuchus	Apollo mates with Coronis and Asclepius is born.
Cancer/Leo	Zeus mates with Alkmene and Herakles is born.
Gemini	Zeus mates with Leda and Polydeuces and Castor are born.
Pisces	Aphrodite mates with Ares. Eros is born.

Scorpio	Orion meets and befriends Hephaistos.
Virgo/Libra	Zeus visits Themis and Astraea.
Cancer/Leo	Herakles is assigned the first of his ten labours.
Cancer/Leo	Herakles befriends Chiron.
Centaurus	Chiron befriends Herakles.
Gemini	Castor and Polydeuces join the Argo crew
Cancer/Leo	Herakles joins Argo crew.
Gemini	Atalanta asks to join Argo crew.
Scorpio	Orion meets Artemis.
Centaurus	Chiron commences as a teacher.
Gemini	Herakles is inadvertently separated from the Argo.
Cancer/Leo	Herakles resumes his labours.
Scorpio	Orion duels with the giant scorpion.
Gemini	Jason and Argo crew return with the Golden Fleece.
Gemini	Calydonian Boar Hunt.
Gemini	Atalanta joins the Calydonian Boar Hunt
Cancer/Leo	Herakles accidentally wounds Chiron
Centaurus	Chiron makes his plea to Zeus.
Pisces	The Greeks and the Trojans start a war that lasts ten years.
Aquarius	Zeus meets Ganymede.
Cancer/Leo	Herakles becomes immortal and marries Hebe.
Pisces	Atalanta competes in a running race against her potential suitors.
Gemini	Castor and Polydeuces become immortal.
Pisces	Aphrodite an Eros escape Typhon.

1

The story of Taurus

The origins on how the first humans came into being has always been a popular discussion topic. Today the evolution from sea to land and from ape to human, seems to be the most widely accepted version, however many people advocate the creation belief. A few people support the notion that our ancestors are descendants from an intelligent species from a distant planet, perhaps one from a galaxy far far away....

The ancient Greeks subscribed to the belief that the first humans, as with all animals, originally grew out from the soil. They had witnessed this event demonstrated by plants and therefore the evidence was compelling. The specific ancient Greek word for this belief is "autochthon," meaning "sprung from the land itself". In its essence, the belief was that those ancient people from within the Greek region were always there, and that they did not just decide to walk in from other places to set up their homes and farms.

This belief gave them a strong sense of interconnectedness with the land and all its bounty. It justified total acceptance of their own reasoning behind everything they saw and experienced. Their rationalising gave credence to the stories they shared to explain everything.

It was also believed that the humans and all the other animals quickly learned to reproduce independently from the soil, and so when we die, we all ultimately return to it. Hence the ritual "we therefor commit this body to the ground, earth to earth, ashes to ashes, dust to dust," that is still often said during burial ceremonies today, as quoted from the Book of Common Prayer.

Whilst ancient Greeks readily believed that humans originally grew up from the soil, they still had to attribute their actual design to someone. They believed that Gaia was their earth mother, and that Zeus was the king of all their gods, but they ascribed the creation of the human form to the Titan Prometheus. He also happened to be Zeus's cousin.

Mythology has it that the first humans to be created were actually commissioned by Zeus's father, Cronus, when he was King of the Titan's. It took Prometheus several attempts before he got it right, and in the beginning only human males were created. He shaped the humans out of clay and water using the same features as the gods themselves. He then gave these human figurines the essence of life.

This all happened long before the Titanomachy, the protracted war between the Titans and the Gods, that ended with the Gods as the victor. Their triumph also positioned Zeus as the new king of all the gods and goddesses.

It was much later that Zeus authorised the first woman to be created. Due to his ongoing displeasure with Prometheus, he assigned that task to his own son, Hephaestus. Her name was Pandora, and her fashioning is another story.

After Pandora, many more women were created, and they quickly equalled the men in numbers. They formed relationships, discovered sex, and soon human population numbers rapidly increased. Humans quickly developed enhanced hunting and gathering skills, and their numbers grew so fast that they could not sufficiently feed themselves by simply hunting and gathering. So, under the guidance from the agricultural gods and goddesses, they developed farming skills and grew grains, vegetables, and fruits, in large enough quantities to feed themselves. They soon introduced crop specialisation, soil improvements, water resource management techniques, crop rotation, bartering, and labour exchange.

It was also during this time that someone had the notion that they could muster and domesticate animals for their meat, and in this way, they could reduce the need to spend time hunting. Some animals were better suited to captivity than others, such as sheep, pigs and goats, and these were marshalled into fields which were rich with their preferred fodder. Fences were erected to hold them captive in one location. Techniques for protecting them from predators, caring for them, and accelerating their yield were learned. Soon, the humans were eating more harvested farmed meat, than meat from the animals they hunted.

The humans, as well as all the other animals that the gods created, were now well on their way to adapting to self-sufficiency and thereby becoming more independent of their gods.

***

Over time, many of the human farmers became dissatisfied with the effort they had to put into producing the meat they currently harvested from the animals that they farmed. It was believed by some men that the effort to meat ratio of their animals was too low. A committee of respected men was established to discuss the problem. They eventually agreed that perhaps they should come up with a design of what they believed was the perfect farm animal. They discussed their current animal breeds, identified their shortcomings, listed what desired improvements they needed to have, discussed height, width, and length of the animal. They even sketched numerous designs of what a better farm animal might look like.

Soon, the men had an acceptable concept. They were confident, resolved, and the designated committee leader decided it was time to meet with the gods to present their plans. This largish beast would improve the quality and increase the quantity their meat supply. It was readily agreed by the men that Prometheus was the obvious god to receive their petition. His reputation for acting on worthy improvements for the benefit of all, was already well established. He was approachable, receptive, respectful, and certainly the most capable.

Now charged with enthusiasm, the committee set off with their drawings and designs of the perfect farm animal, to make their appeal to Prometheus. They knew where to locate him, and he was often accessible without an appointment.

As with many of the gods and goddesses, Prometheus enjoyed his interactions with humans, and he was generally delighted to assist them. Most of the humans he met primped and prepared their finery when planning to consult him. Often, they were asking for ridiculous things and even though these requests amused him, he always responded in a professional and dignified manner.

Humans petitioned the gods and goddesses for many things, and he found himself gratified to be of assistance. Some of the gods and goddesses treated human requests as a nuisance and the humans quickly learned to avoid them. Others were more benevolent and were receptive. Among the gods and goddesses that were helpful to the humans there were two differing beliefs. One group encouraged requests as it kept human's dependent on the gods, and it encouraged vital worshiping and ongoing gratitude. The second group, including Prometheus, used these requests to encourage human learning towards greater self-sufficiency and they saw this current age of problems as mere transitional issues as human's established themselves.

Prometheus's offices were located at the outskirts of the village, and they consisted of a reception area and a conference room. His staff had even set up a separate room where waiting applicants could relieve themselves as public urination was becoming problematic. His human assistants managed to shield him from the troublemakers, and they kept petitioners calm and controlled whilst they waited to speak with Prometheus.

Eventually it was the meat committees turn. The entered his office with something that resembled reverence and trepidation. 'Prometheus, please forgive our intrusion, but we're here to ask for your help,' said the committee leader.

'How can I help you?' Prometheus asked the six human males who now stood before him. He examined them, assessing their backgrounds so he could better understand their application. These six men appeared modest, unpretentious, and they acted sincere. They were dressed in farmers working clothes, and they presented themselves as hardworking honest men of the land.

'Humbly Prometheus, we thank you and the other gods and goddesses for the animals we farm, and for the meat, skins, and wool, that they provide...,' the head man began his introduction. It always amused Prometheus that humans felt that they had to be long winded about introducing a request or a topic. He sometimes wished that they would just get on with it. He once got impatient with a petitioner and urged him to hurry up, but he quickly regretted it, as the man had to re-start his lengthy plea from the very beginning. It seemed that most humans painfully rehearsed their words before coming to see him. '... but we have been talking...' the head man continued, and

Prometheus refocused on his words. '... and we would want, err, to ask for, err, well we need, would like you... to ask you... to create an animal that gives more of itself to us.' He stopped abruptly, relieved to have reached this point. The five other men sighed audibly, each expelling a lungful of air and grateful that the request was now finally out there. They were hopeful, and now seemed expectant that Prometheus would understand, agree, and work-out a way to help them.

'I see,' Prometheus said as he relaxed in his chair. He smiled benevolently toward them, as he knew from experience that this instantly relaxed his human visitors and made them more progressive with their dialogue. 'I suppose in order to achieve more meat you will need a bigger animal.'

'Yes!' chorused the six men. Clearly size mattered.

The men had obviously rehearsed this next part of their presentation. Prometheus suppressed a smile. Their specifications came from all of them, in turn, in segments, as they stood in a neat line before him, with each man looking to the next as soon as he was finished.

'It must be really big, but not too huge, and its body must be bulky and meaty,' explained the first man using his hands to indicate that the beast should be big and heavy.

'Its legs must be sturdy so to support the weight, but not too long so that it can't run fast. We need to be able to catch it when we're ready to butcher it,' added the second using his hands to indicate strength.

'The hair needs to be short so that it doesn't easily get dirty or infested with insects,' explained the third man using his fingers to demonstrate the shortness of the fur.

'Or get tangled,' quipped one man out of sequence.

'The hide must be tough, and waterproof, so that we can reuse the pelts for clothing and footwear, and so we will need to be able to preserve its skin for further use after we've butchered the beast.' He simply nodded to this as if agreeing with his own suggestion.

'The meat needs to be bulky, and it should have a low-fat ratio, but just enough fat so that it is tasty.' This man smiled and seemed to lick his lips in anticipation.

'We want to be able to cook the bones, so that we can make soup and then use them to add flavour when cooking vegetables.' He nodded.

'Do not forget the gravy!'

They laughed and they all relaxed a little as they smiled at each other, clearly pleased with what had been achieved so far.

Prometheus was impressed and feeling somewhat amused by them. He suppressed the urge to chuckle so as to not embarrass his guests. 'What colour to you want this beast to be?' and he hoped their response would be practical.

'Brown is okay,' one man replied.

'Black is also good,' another offered.

'White would make for nice furniture covers,' a third man speculated. 'Perhaps a combination of colours to keep it interesting.'

'So, any colour will be okay, as long as it blends in well with the existing farmed animals coat colourings,' Prometheus concluded for them. 'And how soon do you want these majestic beasts?'

'Now!' they replied in unison nodding vigorously.

'And what will you call it?

The men looked about at each other in embarrassed bewilderment. Their committee had not discussed a name. 'How about calling it, "Gwou"?' someone blurted. They looked about themselves hoping but struggling to come up with a better name.

Prometheus was not convinced that "Gwou" was a good name for the animal that they wanted, and his doubts must have shown on his face. Then someone else suggested "Cow," and they all turned to each other nodding agreement that "Cow" was a good simple name for the simple animal that they were requesting.

'Cow it is,' Prometheus agreed. 'You'll need more than one, won't you?' It was a rhetorical question but typically of humans, they felt compelled to answer it.'

'Yes, Prometheus. We will need them to breed easily so that we can grow their numbers as we need plenty of meat.'

'So, the cows will be females and therefore you will need males in order to produce more cows from them,' Prometheus explained. He was now developing a strong personal interest in this animal.

'Yes, yes. But they must not be too aggressive, as they are in some types of animals. We will also need them to be able to copulate without difficulty or injury.'

'They should be strong, but docile.'

'Perhaps the males could have strong horns so they can protect the cows from wild beasts when we are asleep,' one man suggested.

'That'd be good. You could also use the horns to attach a rope to lead it to where you need it to be,' another agreed. The others smiled and nodded enthusiastically.

'The horns should not be too long. We do not want to get injured by our own food,' a third man lamented.

'Short pointy horns might be good on the cow's also,' a fourth person added to the notion.

Everyone nodded.

'It would be good if they could pull things. We could tie a wagon to it so it could pull heavy loads for us.'

'You could call the male a "Pull Cow," Prometheus suggested.

'No...' The men shook their heads almost comically and Prometheus again suppressed his mirth.

'Bull Cow,' one of the men blurted.

'Or how about we name the females "Cows," and for the males, we will just call them "Bulls"?' He looked about, examining their faces and he was pleased that they were accepting his suggestion.

'Yes! Yes!' the others quickly agreed. Prometheus really liked this committee. Unlike many others he had to contend with, these people clearly had a singular objective and worked well together towards the solution. He was also pleased that they had left any personal agendas at home. He only wished that the gods and goddesses of Mount Olympus could work this well together in such peaceful co-operation. Maybe one day they will find a way to achieve it.

'Anything else you want these cows and bulls to do for you?' Prometheus asked, now excited to get on with the project. The enormous benefit that cows and bulls would have to the humans was obvious to him. Regrettably, because of their potential impact on human advancement, he would need to consult with Zeus about the new animals, as his approval was paramount to these humans achieving their request.

'Milk,' someone said with a tone of modest hope in his voice.

'So that they can suckle their young?' Prometheus clarified the request.

'If the cows can produce more milk than their infants require, then their milk should also be good enough for us to drink. It could become an important food source for us, and over time, we will learn how to make many interesting things to eat from it.' Their head man was clearly intelligent and knowledgeable, and the others were clever enough to have chosen him for the task of leading their committee.

'We make cheese from goats' milk,' one man said.

'I drink goats' milk,' said another.

Prometheus stood up from his chair. 'I am convinced. I can see that this animal will have numerous uses and benefits, I will bet that you'll will even find a use for its excrement,' he said as a joke, but the men nodded and seemed agreeable to the idea, as manures from other animals had already proven beneficial in enriching the soil. 'I will approve your request...' but as he started to explain, they cut him off with a cheer. When they settled, he continued, '...but a project of this magnitude will require some deliberation with Zeus.' The men fell silent. Just when their plan to feed their expanding population seemed to have the support of the gods, Zeus's name came up. Zeus had a reputation for thwarting human progress, and he could easily destroy this plans realisation.

Prometheus studied each man in turn, and he then spoke evenly to all of them. 'Return here in seven days and I will meet with you to discuss my progress with your request.' Prometheus smiled sympathetically at the group. The concept of "the cow", and her male counterpart "the bull", had significant merit. But perhaps it was too much merit for Zeus to be happy with it. He would now have to think of the best way to convince this development to his irascible god king.

The men said nothing. Each in turn bowed toward Prometheus, and they then exited his office in an orderly single file.

***

Prometheus was married to a goddess named Clymene, and together they had a son they named Deucalion. When he got home that night, his wife was delighted to see him so positive about a human request for a new animal. He explained in detail what the potential benefits would be, but his wife was more practical and she only asked him about when could he bring some of the meat home for them to try. Perhaps enough for a barbecue, as they were entertaining soon.

***

The following day, Prometheus set about to arrange a meeting with Zeus. Zeus was generally receptive to seeing him, as long as he did not bring his brother, Epimetheus with him. Epimetheus had a dubious reputation with the gods and goddesses. As the god of hindsight, he tended to have little value to others. Many thought him to be a fool despite his many contributions to creation of the diverse range of animal and plants that inhabited their world.

The brothers one saving grace was that they had sided with the Gods instead of the other Titan's during the Titanomachy, Prometheus had always known that the Gods would be victorious, as he had the gift of prophecy. As Epimetheus often chose poorly when making such decisions, Prometheus had to work hard to convince his brother to fight with Zeus and his family, and not against them. Despite their support for the gods, Prometheus knew their relationship with them, and in particular with Zeus, was still tenuous. Zeus was convinced that as the brothers had switched sides once, then they had the capacity to do so again, and this belief kept him wary of them.

Within the palace on Mount Olympus, where Zeus administered his kingdom, Prometheus was granted an audience with one of Zeus's aides. It was only through him that he was granted a meeting with Zeus the following afternoon. He was invited to attend a popular, and highly respectable eatery, that was situated beside a rocky shoreline. Prometheus knew the place intimately and he was pleased that he was granted an audience with his king well away from all the usual formalities of his palace.

***

Zeus often attended a restaurant by the sea as a venue for his meetings with his brother Poseidon. Zeus poured more wine into his cup. Poseidon pushed his cup toward him indicating that he would like a refill also, to which Zeus happily obliged. The two Gods met in a favoured local eatery for some casual conversation, well away from their respective domiciles. The view from the dining room balcony was impressive with many rocky outcrops providing magnificent vistas for diners to gaze upon whilst they ate. The ocean below them was calm and swell gently undulated, and that reflected Poseidon's current mood, an inward observation that Zeus had made and appreciated.

The eatery was now all but deserted by the other patrons, who upon recognising Zeus and Poseidon, who were trying to appear incognito, were well known and were easily identified, had abandoned their meals and drinks. A seemingly congenial family reunion between these two Gods could quickly turn ugly. Considering the powers that these two gods wielded between them, it was better to leave quickly and avoid becoming collateral damage should an argument ensue. Clearly, they had decided that it was best to leave it to the proprietor to focus on these esteemed patrons.

When the two brothers met informally, it was always by the sea. They would arrive appearing as much like mere mortals as they could. Both were fully aware that if they dressed in their full regal splendour, that it would be fatal for any humans to see them. Zeus could travel anywhere in his kingdom in an instant, but he preferred flying over his realm as a giant eagle. In this way he could spy on human activity and monitor their progress. Poseidon's domain was within the seas and the oceans. Whenever he ventured on land, he preferred to remain in full view of the water. Poseidon rarely visited Mount Olympus as it offered little of interest to him. He generally gave Zeus his proxy vote to use as he wanted in any of the formal Council meetings.

The proprietor delivered yet another jug of wine. There were now two full jugs on the table as he had long ago learned that these gods did not like to be kept waiting. He bowed, and then gathered the empty dishes that had once held their meals. He had often boasted to his regular customers that the meals he served were approved by the gods. He would also add that as long as they were relaxed, he was congenial to have them in his establishment. He bowed his head once more and left them to their conversation. The brothers totally ignored him.

'As you know, I have only been married once,' Poseidon said, continuing their earlier conversation. 'I still am.' He stared at his brother and then added. 'It is true that I only married Amphitrite to shut her up. She said she wanted to bear my child, but she would only do so if we were married and as I was copulating with her during this conversation, I was obviously weak minded. Can you imagine having that discussion whilst in the throes of sex? She lay there looking at me for a response to her marriage proposal, whilst I continued thrusting my way deeper inside of her. Before I realised what I was saying I had agreed, she squealed happily, and for the next few months I had the best sex than I had ever experienced in my whole life!' he sighed. 'As soon as she realised, that she was pregnant, she would not let me near her. When I told her that I was ready for sex, guess what she replied, "help yourself, but not with me." What a girl. Ever since then, I have been doing it with any woman that I have fancied. It has been all pleasure without the care, with no responsibility, and never any recriminations.' Poseidon appeared smug. 'Why do you want to tie yourself down with another wife is a mystery to me.' Poseidon peered into his wine cup and then took another gulp.

Zeus glanced at his brother impassively. They had had this conversation many times before as Poseidon usually comforted his senior brother after one of Zeus's many relationship breakups. Like his brother, he too had often copulated away with impunity, but he had been in real love more times than his oceanic brother. Breakups saddened him. He said nothing.

'I will give you my advice,' Poseidon said with a hint of concern as he reached over to the wine jug and refilled Zeus's cup whilst Zeus watched on. 'Play the field as I do. You have never been shy to get a bit extra on the side when you were married. Now you can do it as a single man. I say go for it. I recently made exquisite love to Theophane on a remote sheepherder's island. I expect that she will soon push out a brat, but so what? Every child should have a father like me.'

Zeus winced. He too had fathered many children. They both had powerful seed. 'But I like being married. It is comforting. Besides, in my role as king, I should have a queen. It gives a sense of balance and order to the other gods and goddesses. Our humans seem to appreciate having a married couple at the helm.'

Poseidon's laughter cut him off. 'It is just that you think sex is more fun when you are cheating!' he concluded and roared in laughter again. 'You need a wife to cheat on, so you can spice up the action.' He looked smug.

'It is not that. It just seems normal to be in that type of union. I like the idea of having a wife, and besides, it really does set a good example to the others.'

'Mother always said that you should never marry. She tried in vain to warn you that marriage would not work out for you. As I recall she even tried to forbid it, but that just made you more determined. Well, now you have had two wives, who were also our aunties, and both of them Titan's, despite the fact that you do not like Titans. So, who is going to be number three?' Poseidon looked expectantly at his brother. He suspected that Zeus had an idea of who his next wife might be and had requested this meeting to get his opinion.

'I wish I knew. What I do know is that this time I want to marry for true love.'

Poseidon roared in laughter again, and Zeus seemed hurt by his reaction. Then they were quiet for a while and examined the empty restaurant without interest, and then they looked out over the sea and took in the magnificent view. They sat for a while in silent contemplation.

It was Zeus who broke the silence. 'I married Metis to gain her loyalty, cunning and wisdom. I should never have had her as a wife as it was wrong from the beginning. Sex was functional and she quickly became pregnant. Then Gaia and Uranus shattered any chance of our happiness by decreeing that her second baby would grow up to attack and dethrone me. Given our family history, I could not let that happen, so I destroyed her. I had sacrificed my wife because of my own insecurity...' Zeus explained, his voice trailing off.

Zeus thought of Metis and his irrational and unforgivable treatment of her. He named a moon in her honour and kept it close to his own planet, memorialising her in the night sky.

'She still managed to give you a beautiful and devoted daughter,' Poseidon offered in comfort.

'Athena is a good girl. She is wise, brave, and only fierce when she needs to be. She is extremely loyal to me, despite her mother's demise by my hand.'

'I think it is because of her mother's fate, that she will never be a challenger to your rule. Athena is too smart to follow her mother into oblivion,' Poseidon observed. Poseidon chose not to bring up the fact that Athena had defeated him in their challenge for the patronage of the human city of Athens. Her gift of olive trees bested his gift of a perpetually flowing spring. Even though the water he provided them was too salty to drink, he was still upset that he had lost.

'Athena might succeed me one day. She is certainly worthy, but I also believe that she will never challenge me. She is not devious like so many of the others,' Zeus concluded, and Poseidon politely nodded his agreement with his brother's assessment.

Zeus next summarised his doomed second marriage. 'I married Themis on impulse. She was sensible, ordered, and organised. I figured she would capably organise me and our kingdom, but she was more interested in organising humans and helping them, than she was ever interested in me, or the affairs of Mount Olympus. I think she only married me because she thought that I'd develop more empathy and interest in encouraging human development under her spousal influence.'

'I believe we need to keep human development in check. It is a good job that you divorced her,' Poseidon agreed. 'Where is Themis now?'

'She is on some island in the middle of the Mediterranean being a do-gooder to the humans. I really must fly out their one day and check-up on her and make sure she is not filling their heads with too many independent notions.'

'You had sex with our sister, Demeter; did you ever think of marrying her?'

Zeus boasted. 'My daughter from her married our brother, Hades.'

'And Hades has never forgiven you.' The brothers laughed heartily.

'You can forget Metis. My daughters with her, like their mother, brought much beauty, grace, and charm into our realm,' Zeus reminisced. 'But she would make a terrible wife.'

'Do you see much of them?' Poseidon never gave much importance to these qualities, unless he was planning to seduce the women that exhibited them.

'Oh, I see them, and I hear about them, but I am not exactly father of the year material. I will never live with my wives, my mistresses, or their children. I am not that kind of father,' Zeus admitted.

'You do seem to have a penchant for our aunts,' Poseidon observed.

'Mnemosyne bragged that she could outperform me sexually. One rises to such a challenge, so we engaged in sex for nine days straight.'

'I am impressed,' Poseidon replied, and he looked it. 'My record is three days, and then I needed a long soak in salty water.'

Zeus roared with laughter at his brother's joke. Poseidon grinned happily and joined in the laughter. He really enjoyed Poseidon's company and instantly regretted that they did not spend more time together. They sighed. 'The only interruption to sex was her delivering a baby. We made nine babies in nine days. That is another record, I am certain of it.'

'How do you remember all their names?' Poseidon looked perplexed.

'I do not,' Zeus confessed, 'and I do not even try. Their names and abilities vary with every telling of their story. We really need someone to properly document all of this. In years to come the details of our lives will confuse students of our culture. Our true heritage will be lost forever.'

'I think not. I like the way story tellers embellish our actions and our deeds. I am entertained by their witticism and insights into our motivations, and the purpose of godly outcomes. If it were written down, the stories about our lives would become static, and we would lose most of the mystical hold that we currently have over the humans.'

'I had not thought of it in that way.' Zeus now looked serious. 'We must discourage humans from writing about us, and only grant the gods of Mount Olympus permission to document who we are, our linage, and our strengths.'

'Not our weaknesses?' Poseidon grinned.

'Perhaps for beautiful women,' Zeus laughed, and Poseidon joined him.

'I once thought that you would marry, Leto. She is only a mortal, I agree, but you did once love her, and still do love your two children from her,' Poseidon said returning the conversation to his brother's immediate problem.

'I have always discouraged mixed marriages. The human rarely copes with our godly actions and skills. Artemis and Apollo are worthy demi-gods, and I have confirmed upon both of them, many skills and powers. They are accepted and respected as immortals and are worthy of their place at Mount Olympus. Their mother, as kind, gentle, and as beautiful as she is, would never survive Mount Olympus. Sadly, I had to let my relationship with her go.'

'So, brother, here you are. You know that your reputation will slow down your romantic pursuits within the kingdom.'

Zeus nodded, but said nothing.

'What about Hera? I am positive that she has always fancied you.'

Zeus shook his head and smiled as he looked at Poseidon. 'I could tell that she was totally sincere, and extremely emphatic, when she explained her feelings about me,' he replied and then using a monotone voice mocking Hera's response to his previous overtures. "I will never marry you, or debauch myself to bed you, even if you were the last god in the kingdom."' Zeus shrugged. 'I understood her declaration.'

Poseidon snorted. 'I suppose she has issues with you and your past relationships.'

'And then some. She likes Athena, and Apollo, but she detests all my other children. I guess Hera is a family orientated kind of woman. She truly believes in the family unit. I said I had changed, and I even promised that we would be happy together, but she will not have it. She said she would rather be single all her life than be married to a deviant womaniser like me.'

'A man is what he is,' Poseidon said defending his brother's actions. They were similar in their treatment of women. 'So, who is next?'

'I do not know,' Zeus admitted. 'I guess I will have to go searching and see if I can meet my perfect woman.'

The proprietor edged closer to the two important guests within his establishment and cleared his throat. 'Please forgive the interruption, but there is a man outside who insists he has an appointment to visit with you,' he explained looking at Zeus. The proprietor appeared nervous, but he stood his ground waiting for his response.

Zeus stared at the man and then he remembered. He said to Poseidon, 'That must be Prometheus. I told him to meet me here, I hope you do not mind?' Poseidon shook his head. He turned back to the proprietor. 'Invite him to join us and bring him some food and wine,' Zeus commanded. The man bowed and withdrew. Soon the statuesque, handsome, and well-dressed Prometheus entered the room and warmly greeted both Zeus and Poseidon. This Titan had earned his place among the Gods and was respected. Zeus sometimes felt Prometheus had too much empathy for humans, and he intentionally kept this powerful Titan close by so he could be watched and curtailed as needed.

'Thank you for agreeing to meet with me,' Prometheus started respectfully. He still feared Zeus's power and retribution, but he was here on an important mission that would benefit the gods and humans alike. 'This venue is the perfect place for my presentation.'

'I am happy we could accommodate. What's on your mind?' Zeus asked inviting the Titan to explain why he wanted this meeting.

'I've arranged a demonstration,' Prometheus replied smiling and signalled to the proprietor to bring in the food that he had arranged to be prepared. The proprietor carefully delivered three platters. One contained cooked mutton, the next cooked goat, and the third held an assortment of cooked seafood. He bowed and retreated.

'I hope you are hungry Prometheus, as we have already eaten.' Zeus tried not to appear ungrateful.

'This is for demonstration purposes,' Prometheus explained. 'These meats represent the meat we normally eat...' Poseidon seemed to agree by delving into the seafood platters as if famished. '... I propose another beast, one which I will create, that will have a stronger flavour of meat, it will be a reddish grey colour, and it will come from an agreeable and manageable beast. It will produce a high yield of quality meat. It'll also produce large volumes of milk for drinking and for cheese making.'

'That would seem impressive,' Zeus decreed, and he looked it. He turned to his brother who did not seem impressed. Then he remembered that Poseidon's passion was for seafood and watched him as he happily took another handful into his mouth.

Prometheus was pleased that Zeus agreed his plan had merit. Without Zeus's approval he would not dare to proceed. 'The skin will also make fabulous material for clothing and shoes. We can even make soup from its bones.'

'Prometheus, you've hit a winner with this one. You have my approval. What do you plan to call this meat?'

'I plan to call the female beast a "cow" and the male a "bull"'.

'How did you come up with this idea?' It was Poseidon who queried the Titan.

Prometheus hesitated. He was not sure how Zeus would react to learning that the plans for the cow and the bull were designed by a committee of humans. He tried hard to appear indifferent as he explained. 'I have designed many animals. Many are for sport, but mostly they are for food, so the cow and the bull are merely an extension of my work.'

When can we try this meat?' Zeus had already moved on as Poseidon was busily consuming the remnants of the seafood platter.

Prometheus was keen to start straight away, and he was encouraged by Zeus's enthusiasm. 'I should have a walking model quite soon,' he ventured without committing himself. 'After I have done some trials, I will present the finished beast to you for your approval.'

'Make the bull a bit feisty, so it can protect its females against predators. Give it some fighting instincts, but not so much as to allow it to damage its own flesh.'

Prometheus nodded agreement, stood, bowed, and left the table and exited the eatery.

'Cows and Bulls,' Zeus muttered. 'Progress hey?' Zeus glanced at his brother.

'They probably won't catch on,' Poseidon replied doubtfully. 'But if it does, I think I will need a sea version of the cow and her bull.'

***

The following morning, Zeus morphed once more into his giant eagle form and took to the skies. He was determined that this time he would meet a wonderful woman, and that they would fall deeply in love with each other. He wanted mutual commitment. She needed to be refined, educated, beautiful, respected, and above all else she should be willing to enthusiastically and happily reciprocate his many physical affections. He told himself that he would not use trickery this time to seduce this woman, and that he would remain true to her always. He wanted her in such a way that she would love him for him, and not because he had manipulated her into the relationship. Zeus was feeling confident that this honest, truthful, and noble approach would reward him with the perfect wife, and that he would achieve everlasting and unconditional love.

Zeus understood that he was feeling romantic, hopeful, anxious, and out of his depth by the prospect of starting a genuine relationship, all at the same time. He hoped a solution would present herself soon.

He flew the clear skies for many days, remaining forever vigilant in the hope of finding and meeting the woman of his dreams. He was relaxed and comfortable in his eagle form, and from up high he could better grasp the enormity of his kingdom. Being a sky god gave him powers over the clouds, wind, and the rain, and for this purpose he required a clear visage over his domain. The sky was a vivid blue, and Helios reliably lit up his world. Zeus enjoyed watching over the humans as they stumbled through their daily routines. They amused him.

It was late on the third day of flying that he spotted a beautiful young woman who was picking flowers from a garden. He landed close by, morphed, and walked to a spot where he could observe her discreetly.

She was dressed in a summer frock that contoured her firm body magnificently. The fabric was skin toned and at first, he had thought that she was naked, and he had to admit that this prospect was the first thing that had attracted him to her. Closer inspection yielded positive results. Her face radiated youthful innocence. Her skin, though a little pale, was clean and unblemished. Her breasts, though well covered, were firm and perfectly proportioned and they were pleasing to look at. Her hair was clean and lush and was a golden brown and it was restrained by hair clips. Her tall slender body made her appear athletic, and Zeus felt an immediate attraction, and so he decided that he would like to learn more about her.

'I can see that you are watching me,' she said to him. Her voice did not portray alarm or even concern. She merely let him know that his attempt at seeing her unobtrusively, had failed. He stepped away from the tree that he had been hiding behind, but he did not move toward her as he did not want to alarm the young woman. His own attire was simple, and he presented himself as a businessman. He appeared to carry no weapons, although that was never true.

Zeus spoke in soft tones to assure the woman that she was in no danger. 'I am sorry if I caused you any concern. It is just that you are strikingly beautiful, and I wanted to learn more about you before I approached.'

'Do you always stalk your prey in this way?' her voice was kind.

He smiled. 'I am not stalking you; it is just that I was a little concerned that you may have been underaged for a man of my, er...' he stalled not wanting to admit that he was much older than she was.

'Tastes?' she ventured.

'Yes! Of a man of my tastes. I would prefer meeting a woman with some experience.'

'So, virgins are not your thing? Then I am sorry for you, as I have chosen to remain one, and therefore you are out of luck.'

'Is that a lifelong commitment?' he asked. He knew of women that had foolishly vowed abstinence.

'No silly. I am saving myself for my future husband.' She studied him. 'Are you a man of many conquests, or are you also saving yourself for your bride?'

Zeus could tell that she was baiting him. He was somewhat flummoxed by her. She was young, but also seemingly confident in conversation. He drew in a deep breath and tried to explain. 'You see, I am a lonely man that is seeking a female companion with a view to a permanent and lasting relationship.'

'And so, you thought you would try with me?'

'You seem like an interesting woman, so, I came closer, hoping to meet you…' he started walking nearer to her, 'and so that I could see you better.' He stopped when he was just out of arms distance. She was even prettier up close, and he was pleased with himself for making the effort. 'Every relationship has to have a starting point.'

'You really should get to know me first before you start planning our relationship.'

'Yes, of course,' he agreed laughing. 'As I am already enjoying your company, I think we are getting off on a good start,' he explained, and then paused to gauge her response. She said nothing and remained expressionless. As there was none, he continued. 'Would you be interested in getting to know me a little better also?'

'You could start by telling me your name,' she admonished.

'Of course, my name.' He smiled. 'I am known to all as "Zeus,"' he said as he bowed.

She burst into laughter.

'What is so funny?' he was confused and a little taken back. No one had laughed at his name before.

'Zeus! Your parents decided to name you after the great king of the gods himself. That was somewhat pretentious.'

'I, er…' he stumbled, unsure of how to respond.

'I already know several Zeus's, two Poseidon's, and even a Prometheus. Why cannot parents be more original when choosing names for their children?'

It had not occurred to him that humans might name children after their gods. He always believed that his name was a mighty godly name, and that it was his alone. He now wondered how many Zeus's there were in the human world. He suddenly felt uncomfortable about sharing his name with mortals. Other gods knew better than to imitate him, but it seemed that human's had fewer boundaries.

He decided that he did not want to correct her. Perhaps some anonymity for now was the better part of valour. This part of the dating ritual always seemed to him to be a battle of wits. He suddenly felt that he was out of his depth, despite his numerous conquests and sexual liaisons. This pretty young female was too assertive for him, and he was not sure that he liked it. He did not mind a relationship challenge, but he did not want and amorous contest. He would pursue the right woman with both his heart and his mind, but it did not need to be a contest, well, at least not this time.

'My parents had mixed feelings about the gods,' he explained. He knew his response was both accurate and yet cryptic.

'Mine taught me to be respectful of them. I think my parents are a bit older than you are,' she concluded after examining his features.

Zeus had involuntarily drawn in his breath and had expanded his chest and pulled in his abdomen under her scrutiny. He now felt silly and relaxed. As a god he could morph his physical appearance into any shape or age that he wanted to appear. He now realised that he was trying too hard to impress this young woman. He should have made himself younger before he stepped forward, but then he was trying to approach the task of finding true love in a genuine and honest way.

'I do not think my parents would approve of you,' she concluded.

'Is that an issue?'

'Not really.'

'Is your father a warrior?'

'No!'

'An important leader?'

'No. He is just a merchant. He seems to be exceptionally good at it. My brothers all work for father and we all have a comfortable life.'

'And you?'

'I help mother. We do not have any interest in father's business. I will be married off soon and I will start my own family.'

Zeus relaxed. He was beginning to feel hopeful. 'How should we continue this...? I mean how do we get to know each other better?'

'Perhaps you should invite me to have a meal with you,' she suggested and glanced at him for his response. He nodded and so she continued. 'In the village there is an eatery named "The Roasted Piglet." If you would like to know me better, we could meet there and have supper together, and then you can tell me all about yourself and your parents.' She smiled and came closer to him and reached up to stroke his beard. 'You never know, I might even decide that I like you, just a little.' She smiled, flashed her eyes mischievously, and then turned and started to walk away.

'What is your name?' he called after her.

She turned and smiled warmly at him. 'I am Elixia, and I am twenty-one years old.' She performed a quick wave goodbye, turned, and then continued walking away.

Elixia. That is a pretty name for a pretty young woman, thought Zeus as he watched her, admiring her from behind. He began to imagine himself being intimate with this woman, but then chastised himself, as his mission was for the mature long-term pursuit of true love, and not for the short-term act of lust.

He thought of morphing into his eagle's form once more, but he decided to rest for a while. Helios was still high in the sky, and it would be some time before he would meet with Elixia for their meal and conversation. He found a comfortable bed of grass under the shade of a tree and laid down. Before too long, he was in a deep sleep.

***

When Zeus woke up, Helios was now just over the horizon. He morphed once more into an eagle and flew closer to the settlement. When he landed, he surveyed the scene. When he was satisfied that he had arrived unobserved, he expediently changed into his human form, and he then confidently stepped out and into the throng of human activities. It seemed that today was market day, and the place was busy with stalls with vendors offering fruits, vegetables, livestock, farming equipment, clothing, jewellery and trinkets, ready to eat foods, toys, and other amusements.

The villagers seemed content. They were adequately dressed and relatively clean. Their banter was lively, and it appeared that the business of buying and selling was robust in this community. There were musicians and street entertainers, who for the promise of coins, performed impromptu melodies, songs, and danced to delight the crowds. Zeus smiled at the revellers and concluded that this was a productive settlement and he admired and respected the locals for their prosperity.

Zeus also noted that the security staff, though present, remained unobtrusive but accessible.

After walking the length of several of the main streets, he finally found the restaurant that Elixia had nominated for their meeting. "The Roasted Piglet," seemed clean and well patronised. It had stone walls and a fixed roof and unlike many eateries, it appeared like it had been constructed for its purpose. He smelt the aromas of roasting boar meat emanating from the open door and realised that he was hungry. He also decided that he would like a cup of wine. He entered the building, found a table with two chairs next to the wall which was adjacent to a window. He sat down and looked outside, but he could not see her.

Zeus next surveyed the room. Most of the chairs were occupied. Some patrons were eating, many were drinking wine or beer. All of them seemed prosperous, seemed happy, and they contentedly engaged in lively conversations. Zeus was satisfied that his presence did not attract any undue curiosity, and so he relaxed. There was a mixture of men and women, but not too many young children. It was a pleasant eatery with more than the usual ambience.

He was about to summon a waiter to order some wine for himself when he wondered if Elexia drank wine... perhaps he should wait, as if he ordered wine for her and she did not like it, she might think that he was trying to intoxicate her. That might make her suspicious of his intentions and he wanted this meeting to go well. He next laboured over what to say when she arrived. Should he stand when she approached, was that the thing to do to be respectful, or did that make him appear old fashioned or possibly even too formal. He then felt that he was over thinking meeting her and he shook his head to tried to clear his mind. He decided he would just relax and watch the other patrons for a while. He drew in a deep breath and exhaled slowly. He smiled at the realisation that he was nervous and that this was a rarity for him.

He was looking forward to seeing her and he hoped that she would arrive soon as the smells of the food and drink was having a gnawing effect on his appetite. The proprietor gave him the look that suggested that he had better order something soon or vacate the table. They were getting busier, and people wanted to sit down and order their meals.

Just then, a woman stepped up to him and asked, 'Are you, Zeus?'

She was a good-looking woman. Zeus estimated her age to be in her late thirties. Her figure was well proportioned, and her clothing indicated a level of refinement. Her skin and features revealed a woman with both the means and the time to take care of herself. She was no servant, farm hand, or scullery maid.

'I am,' he replied as he presented her with his benevolent boyish grin. He hoped she did not recognise him as the god Zeus, and that she was simply a messenger from Elexia.

'May I sit down?' she asked politely.

Zeus nodded and indicated the chair and she sat before him. The woman turned and signalled to the proprietor, evidently, she knew him. Expediently, two cups of wine were served to them by one of the staff who smiled knowingly at the woman.

She held up the cup in salute and so Zeus did the same. They nodded and sipped wine from their cups and then slowly placed their cups onto the table. He waited patiently while she drew in a breath and calmly spoke. 'My name is Marina, and I am Elexia's aunt.'

'Is she okay?'

'Oh, she is fine.' She shook her head dismissively. 'She sends her apologies as she won't be joining you for a meal tonight, or any other night.'

'Did her father forbid her?'

Marina laughed. 'Heavens no. Elexia is an independent woman. A bit head strong and decidedly self-determined. Trust me, if Elexia wanted to be here, then she would be. She told me that she did want to meet with you when she proposed the arrangement, but sorry for you, she now does not.'

'Oh,' Zeus replied, not knowing what to think or say.

'Do not take it too badly. You see, she is betrothed, but until just recently she was not all that confident that she loved her fiancé.'

'But now she does? What changed?'

'You. It would seem that you have helped her to decide her fate. Aren't you a wonderful man? In your pursuit of a woman half your age, you gave her much-needed clarity, where before she only had confusion.'

Zeus decided that he was not adversely affected by this new development. Nothing between them had actually ignited, and as she was so much younger than he wanted his wife to be, it was perhaps for the best. 'Then I am happy for her,' he conceded and smiled reassuringly to Marina.

'The food here is excellent. Shall we order?'

Marina was attractive and well spoken. Zeus decided that she was actually a step up from the too youthful Elexia. He concluded that spending some quality time with this more mature woman might be both pleasant and opportunistic. 'Yes, I am famished. Please order for both of us, as I am sure that you have local knowledge of what is palatable.'

She flashed him a confirming smile and turned once more to the proprietor. Her silent communication with him was sufficient to arrange food and more drinks. They were promptly served.

Zeus stared out the window when he heard a sudden wind gust. The leaves and other discarded items suddenly blustered about. As they settled, Zeus watched the wind suddenly morph into a human form. Despite the mass of human activity, no one noticed the manifestation. Zeus had an inward smile at the power of the gods. As he watched he recognised that it was Zephyrus, the god of the west wind. Zephyrus looked straight at Zeus. The look on his face was one of instant recognition, and so naturally Zephyrus did what any curious god would do. He advanced toward Zeus to find out why he was here and what he was up to. But Zeus imperceptibly motioned for the wind god to go away, and Zephyrus knew how to be discreet, and so he veered away to carry on with his original purpose for visiting. Zeus did not know or care what that was, he was only relieved not to be identified by this well-intentioned wind god.

Marina interrupted his thoughts. If she was aware of Zeus's exchange with Zephyrus, she gave no indication or concern. Marina decided to start the conversation. 'So, I hear that you are a merchant, and that you are hoping to meet a woman who will one day become your wife?'

'Yes, to both,' Zeus replied. 'Are you married?'

She shrugged. 'I was, but he was killed. Like my brother and yourself, my late husband was a merchant. He was traveling between villages when he and his team were set upon by bandits. Events took a turn for the worse when he foolishly decided to defend his merchandise.'

'And he was fatally attacked,' nodded Zeus knowingly.

'It seems that swords are more deadly than knives even when accompanied with well-chosen words. My husband and his men were outnumbered and outmatched. They were slain and left in a ditch beside the road.'

'I am sorry for your loss,' Zeus said, and he found himself feeling genuinely bad for what had happened to her husband. Law and order were mostly mortal matters and only a few of the gods involved themselves with the humans in matters of law enforcement and justice. 'Were the perpetrators found and punished?'

'No,' Marina replied visibly upset. She drew in a deep breath and continued. 'I loved him very much.'

'You must miss him terribly,' Zeus concluded.

'I did at first, but the tragic reality of life is that it ends. For some it ends prematurely, and those remaining are left to deal with the consequences. I was fortunate to have my family to support me emotionally. I feel I am now ready to move on with my life.'

'Families are important,' Zeus agreed.

'Tell me about yours,' she instructed.

I have two brothers and three sisters. We are not close and all of us are estranged from our parents. There is really not much to tell,' Zeus suddenly felt melancholic.

'Have you ever been married?'

Twice, but my first wife died soon after giving birth to a girl. For my second wife, well, it seemed that we were great friends, and we certainly respected each other, and the sex was fantastic, but we eventually realised that we did not actually love each other.'

'Did you have any children with your second wife?'

'Ah, no.'

'How old is your daughter?'

'She is an adult and lives independently from me. I love her and she loves me, but she is a liberated and self-determined woman and I respect her for that,' Zeus explained and he hoped that it was enough detail to satisfy Marina's curiosity about Athena. He desperately wanted to avoid mentioning her name, as Athena was a popular goddess, and Marina would quickly link her to Zeus, King of all the Gods. Zeus was not ready to reveal that titbit of information.

'Love is a difficult concept,' Marina added as she nodded her understanding of his lament.

'In my younger days, when I was adventurous and lustful, love was all about the physical attraction. I would believe that I was in love with a woman, but it was not my mind or my heart that was doing the actual convincing.'

Marina laughed.

Zeus continued. 'I then began to believe that love had to involve an emotional attachment. For love to exist beyond the desire, there needs to be additional connections.'

'Such as?'

'Affection, concern for safety and wellbeing, regards for other possessions, consideration for the other persons needs for emotional and material things, respect is exceptionally important, mutual values, shared goals, the freedom to express ideas without fear of retribution, just to name a few.'

'True love is unconditional.'

'To a point.'

'Missing them when you are apart is also a sure sign of love.'

'Yes, it is true that absence makes the heart grow more desperate to be together. It would be nice to have someone to miss. I admit that I am lonely, and that I would really like to meet someone special to share my life.'

'But you are a merchant. You must meet many attractive women as you do your trade.'

'Meeting women is not my issue. Meeting the perfect woman for me has been my challenge.'

'Maybe you expect too much,'

Zeus pondered her point. Did he expect too much? A woman would need to be quite remarkable to be any match for him. He was the king of all the gods and goddesses of Mount Olympus. He had supreme powders over everything and everyone, and here he was masquerading as a humble merchant trying to find a new wife to share his life. Would a mortal woman cope with his lifestyle. He did not know what to think, but he was willing to continue learning more about Marina, especially as she seemed worldly, experienced, and she certainly was attractive.

'Have I upset you?' she asked, and she reached out to touch his hand.

He did not pull his hand away, but he turned it palm upwards to show that he appreciated her touch. He softly squeezed her fingers. 'No,' he assured her calmly. 'I was just in a moment of self-reflection. The last few years of my life have led me to want to reevaluate my understanding of who I truly am.'

She smiled as she pulled away and sat upright. 'You are a merchant. You travel the country to make deals and profits. You are fiscally motivated.'

That was true of his alter ego, but it was not true of himself. He smiled at her conclusion. 'Money isn't everything.'

'Tell that to my brother. What do you sell? Is it general merchandise, or do you specialise?'

'Rugs.'

'My brother specialises in rugs and floor coverings. His come from Libya. Where do your rugs come from?'

'Persia.'

'We do not see many Persian rugs here.'

'The quality of my rugs is exceptional as they are manufactured by the finest craftsmen. But I do seem to be out-priced by your brother. It is no wonder that I am not selling much in these parts, as his Libyan rugs are cheaper.'

'Only the wealthy can afford Persian rugs. It is a limited market,' she agreed knowingly.

'I had better move on,' Zeus concluded trying to appear sad at the prospect of leaving.

'I will talk to my brother. Perhaps you can collaborate and share the market with him and you will both profit from the partnership. He is entrepreneurial, so I am sure he will find a way to make it worth your while. You may have business connections in Persia that can offer us products that are more in demand.' She smiled and seemed excited at the prospect of Zeus being in her life.

Zeus realised that Marina was giving him a reason to stay. She was inviting him to make a familiar connection with her family. Maybe her interest in him was becoming reciprocal.

He leaned forward. 'I would like that. Thank you. And I would like to spend more time with you also.' He then reached out to hold her hand again. She smiled and reciprocated, both of them feeling a glowing warmth from this new level of intimacy.

Suddenly she pulled back and indicated to the bar staff that they needed more wine. When it arrived, she held up her cup in salute. 'To the happy times that await both of us.'

Zeus returned the salute and smiled as he nodded. 'And, may there be plenty of them.'

They sipped from their cups.

'I really like you Zeus. I am so glad that I came here to meet with you.' She smiled warmly at him, which he happily returned.

Zeus was now beginning to think that the timing was right to tell her who he actually was. He had experienced the consequences of his deceptions in the past, and he understood that if he maintained them for too long that it could go bad for him. He was feeling comfortable with her, and hoped that the truth about his identity did not spoil what they had already achieved.

Marina then suddenly sat upright and stared pensively at him. 'It is a pity about your name. Would you consider changing it?' she asked hopefully.

'My name?'

'Yes. I think you are such a nice person, and I find myself attracted to you, despite your messed up past. You seem genuine and kind, and I would really like to get to know you better,' Marina explained.

'I would like that also. I believe you to be a fine woman, and I am really enjoying your company.' He paused, drew in a deep breath and continued. 'But you do not like my name. You do understand that I've become quite attached to it.' He tried to smile to make light of this deteriorating development.

'It is just that..., well, you see..., every time from now on when I think of you, I want it to be about the warm, compassionate, handsome man that you are. But when I think of you by your name, I am immediately thinking about the king of the gods.'

He nodded his understanding. He then started to explain with some hesitation in his voice. 'Listen…, about Zeus… let me…'

'I believe him to be a disgusting piece of work,' she said cutting him off. Her voice betrayed obvious resentment and bitterness.

'You do not like the king of the gods?' Zeus searched about the room as if concerned that she would get into trouble with the other patrons for being so disrespectful.'

'Do not worry. He is not popular here.' She laughed and leaned forward to reassure him. 'We can speak freely.'

'Are all of the gods so unpopular?' Zeus tried hard to contain his surprise and disbelief.

'Mostly it is Zeus that I do not like. He is the worst of them.'

'Can I ask why?'

'Do you approve of his behaviours?' Marina challenged.

'No, well yes, I suppose I do; it is just that he is the king of the gods and he has so much power. I guess I just imagined that everyone respected and worshiped him.'

'Not many do around these parts. I suggest you keep your assessment about "Zeus the god" to yourself.'

Zeus was in shock. He was not sure how to proceed. His previous feelings for Marina were rapidly dissipating and he felt the urge to exit the building with some haste, or otherwise he may prove her right.

Marina took his quietness to mean that he was beginning to realise that his faith in Zeus the god was misguided. She allowed him his personal reflective moment about what she was saying. He then looked at her as if to indicate that he did not understand and that she should continue.

To her, he now seemed to be lost and bewildered. She felt immediately sorry for devaluing his faith, but she felt confident enough to want to expel his misguided beliefs about Zeus to him. She tried to maintain an explanatory calming voice when describing the king of the gods' poorer qualities. 'You see, your namesake is terribly irresponsible when it comes to others. He rarely considers the consequences of his actions, and he often acts on a whim.'

'I see,' he replied, but he did not.

'I have friends who have worked at Mount Olympus, and they tell me that he can be surly and bordering on aggressive, and that he often has bursts of rage and extreme violence.'
'I think he would have valid reasons for any actions or retributions.'

'Possibly, but given his powers, the terms overuse and disproportionate comes to mind. He is not a forgiving god. He is a pathological liar and he is well-practiced at deceit and subterfuge.'

Zeus was taken back by this strongly worded accusation. Despite the fact that it had a major element of truth to it, he was suddenly feeling uncomfortable. He did not realise that human's felt that way about him. He also knew that it was now unlikely that he would confess that he was not just a traveling carpet salesman.

Marina continued. 'He expertly uses his superficial charm to manipulate women into having sex with him, with no regard for the consequences. I hesitate to think of the number of children he has fathered, or the number of women who were left to fend for themselves after he ruined their lives. He has a captivating appeal before the act, and no empathy after the deed is done.'

Zeus thought she was making it sound worse than it was, but he said nothing. He felt that there was some truth in what she said, but now felt that he was being chastised like some hormone driven recalcitrant male youth. Inwardly, he was feeling just a little remorseful, but outwardly he managed to portray a stoic expression of impassiveness.

Marina continued unabated. 'He makes no attempt to understand others feelings. He only cares about himself.' She drew in a deep breath. 'It is all about him, his needs, his authority, his claim on everything and everyone.'

Zeus could not fully agree with that assessment, and also drew in a deep breath and was about to object, and try to somehow explain his benevolence. He wanted to tell her about the council of Gods and all the good work they were doing to help and assist human progress. But the look on her face dissuaded him and so he turned away, crestfallen. He now felt like a troubled and deluded god whose bad behaviour was being exposed, and that he was now being admonished.

Zeus performed a small inward smile. It suddenly occurred to him that he could prove her right by leveling this place and killing everyone inside of it. But he refrained as he knew deep down that he would not like to have the memory of doing that, so he sat in sulky silence.

'So will you change your name?' Marina asked smiling as she sensed that he now fully appreciated her ill feelings about Zeus the God, and that she now wanted Zeus the carpet salesman to disassociate with him.

'You have giving me much to think about Marina,' Zeus explained. He was soft spoken.

'I have spoilt the mood, I am sorry,' Marina spoke and her voice was now sad. Her face contorted into a grimace.

Zeus answered her with his silence. He forcibly sniffed the air.

'Have a think about what I said. If you want to find me, ask for me at my brother's carpet warehouse. They will know where to find me.' She stood up. Walked around the table and leaned down to kiss him, but it landed on his cheek. Finding that he did not reciprocate, she felt disappointed, but she was not sorry. She did not want a relationship with a man that reminded her of a god she did not like or trust.

Marina left the building and Zeus had wordlessly let her go. He sat in silence for a long while. Romance was at his table tonight, but it had escaped. There were no witnesses. He was Zeus the god, and not just a humble Persian carpet salesman. His life was at Mount Olympus and he was both feared and respected. He still wanted to find true love, but he knew that it would not be with Marina. He would reflect deeply on all the things she had listed about him. A part of him recognised that she was accurate in her assessment of him, and that she had hurt his feelings, just a little. He wondered if this discussion with Marina would alter his future behaviours. Would it affect his destiny when romantically dealing with women, or the other gods, and of the humans generally? He did not yet know the answers.

Zeus stood up from the chair that he had occupied for the evening. Many of the other patrons had already cleared the room as it was getting late. He sought out some coins that approximated the cost of the meals and the wine, and dropped them noisily onto the table. He nodded at the proprietor, and then calmy exited the building into the cold dark night.

***

Zeus awoke to find Helios shining brightly on his face. He had slept in a field and was feeling the strain from sleeping rough. He rolled on his back and thought of his encounter with Marina. He was sorry for the way it went, but he was resolved to turn the loss into something salvageable. It would not be with Marina, that opportunity was now gone forever, but Zeus resolutely measured his life, not by his setbacks, but what he did as a consequence of those temporary disappointments.

He walked back into the village, but his desultory mood prevailed. He found a place to eat, which he did without enthusiasm, and he generally moped about the village unsure of what to do next. His melancholic mood left him feeling tired and apprehensive on how to proceed. Marina's admonishment still echoed in his mind. She exposed him on so many levels it was difficult to process it all. As he pondered his next move he saw Zephyrus once more. He was tempted to learn of the wind gods purpose for being here, but then he decided not to.

Zeus, the King of the Gods, now decided that Zeus, the carpet merchant, was a bad idea and that he would abandon that persona. He would be honest and find true love by being himself. He would become Zeus the benevolent god, the one who respected others, listened and empathised with their problems and issues. He would be the god that was kind, compassionate, and generous. He would use his powers for good, and he now wanted to be a better man for having experienced Marina's assessment of him. True, it hurt to learn that his humans felt that way about him. So, he now decided that the experience was a good one after all, and that it would lead him to present himself as a better god, and more importantly, a worthy candidate for a suitable marriage. Zeus then decided that he would depart from this place and fly to the next village to resume his search for the perfect woman to become his wife. He would leave Zeus the carpet salesman behind.

After a long flight, Zeus landed, morphed, and then proceed into the village. He made certain that he had put enough distance so that it was unlikely he would be recognised by anyone who saw him at the other settlement. He found a table at an eatery and sat down. He summonsed the waiter and ordered food from a list of meals on offer. He also bought a cup of wine and asked for a jug of water.

As he waited for his food, a stunningly beautiful brunette-haired woman with flawless pale white skin came and sat on his lap. She held his face and then kissed him fully on the mouth. He felt her press her breasts into him and she moved rhythmically on his lap. Despite the weight of her on his groin, he felt the pangs of lust rise within him. He disengaged from her mouth.

'You are an amazing kisser,' she whispered into his ear.

'Do you have someplace that we could go to, to get to know each other better?' he asked hopefully.

'Only if you have the coin to pay for it?' she said smoothly.

'The room, or you?' he was puzzled.

'Well, both my darling. Everything costs money. It makes the world go round.' She smiled warmly at him.

'I thought that it was love that made the world go round?' he challenged.

'Of course it does sweetie. You can call it whatever you like.'

Zeus had never "paid" for sex in his entire life. This woman was really turning him on and perhaps the release from recent frustrations would be good for him. He considered the option, but was not yet convinced.

'Honey, time is money. Do you want some action?' she asked as she wriggled some more on his lap. His member was now fully erect and he was feeling considerably uncomfortable. She had a persuasive technique, but he decided to reject her offer, and to save himself for someone with whom he could enjoy intimacy as a part of a meaningful and loving relationship.
'Instead of sex, can I pay you to have a conversation with me?'

She seemed disappointed. 'It is your money honey. Pay me by the hour, and you can do whatever you like with it.'

'How much?'

'Less than you can afford. I am not cheap, but you appear to be a man of wealth and influence.'

Her flattery made him smile. He decided he did not want to know her name. He looked outside for inspiration and saw roses growing in a flower bed. 'Will my money buy me the right to call you "Rose" for the hour?'

'Oh, honey, that's perfect,' she gushed. 'That is my name. You are so clever and...' she felt his arms, 'so... very... strong. You are a very handsome man and I will bet that you are an amazing lover. How would you like to show me how skillful you are? I would be ever so grateful.'

His eyes widened as he stared at her, and he saw her smile innocently. He admitted to himself that her methodology for seduction was flawless. He was certain that she could charm the pants off of any man she set her sights on.

'Shall we go?'

She slid off his lap and held out her hand. He reached for it, but she pulled it away. 'No silly. I will need my money, upfront.'

He nodded his understanding. He wondered how many men had fled after the deed was done and before paying her. He thought that it probably was only one. All of her clients would make payment before sampling her affections. He reached into his pocket and emptied it into her cupped hands. 'How much of your time will that buy me?'

She examined his meagre offering. 'Not much, but as you do not want sex, we can save time and some of your coins by staying here to...' she drew in a deep breath, 'just talk.'

She turned and headed to the bar and reached for a jug of wine and then grabbed two cups. She dropped the coins into a bowl and nodded at the proprietor. She had clearly done this before and she was good for his business.

'What is on your mind, honey?'

'Well, Rose, what can you tell me about love?'

'Oh, sweetie,' she said, seemingly sorry for him. 'I have given up on love a long time ago. It is lucky for me that I enjoy sex. Not many of the girls in our line of work do, you know. Oh, they will tell every client that they are the greatest and most satisfying man that they have ever been with, and funnily enough, some of the men actually believe them.' She laughed at the absurdity of male naivety.

'Have you ever been in love?'

'I loved my mother. It was my father that put me into this line of work, so I am not so keen on him.'

'I meant, have you ever been in love in a traditional way?'

'A few of my regulars have proffered their undying love to me, but they did not have much else to offer. I long ago decided that I was much better off working on my back rather that getting involved with a man that would want sex for free. Getting paid for doing it seems to me to make it more exciting. Are you sure that you do not want me? I've got a good feeling about you.'

Zeus shook his head. He should have realised that a sex worker would be good at talking about sex and would probably have little regard for true love. He was beginning to think that he was wasting his time with Rose, or whatever her name was. He was beginning to doubt his judgement. Perhaps Marina was correct in her unkind assessment of him. He inwardly winced at that possibility.

'My sister found true love. She married a kind man. He's a bit older than she is but she keeps telling me that he is a good husband. They have two children now. I am an aunty.' She smiled at this. 'I sometimes take a break from sex and go have a holiday with them. I keep my occupation a secret because her husband would not approve, and it might confuse their children. I've got a feeling my sister has worked out what I do, because she has always been good at figuring me out, but she doesn't say anything, and so we do not talk about how I earn my money.

Zeus nodded his understanding.

Rose continued. 'She gushes about how nice he is and that he brings her flowers from the garden, and she says that he is always polite and considerate. He always has charming things to say to her, or about her to others, not just because he's horny, but because he likes making her feel loved and valued. Isn't he wonderful? He carries heavy things for her and he even rubs her feet when they are weary. He always listens to what she has to say, and they even make the important decisions together. Can you believe that? Anyway, she seems delighted to be with him, and I am just happy for her. Even her children are gorgeous, polite, and well behaved.' She stopped abruptly. After a pause she stared at Zeus and then continued. 'I guess, if I ever end up meeting the right man, I might like to start a family of my own. The trouble is that you do not really know what type of man you are getting until it is too late. Many women end up married and bound for life to the beast, before they get to realise that they actually married a loser, or even worse, a basher.'

Zeus nodded knowingly, but still said nothing.

'So, honey, there you have it.' She smiled at him. 'You are a good listener; did you know that?' Zeus raised his eyebrows questioningly. 'Have you got your monies worth, sweetie? I hope so. You seem like a decent fellow. I am sure you will find true love someday. Keep searching and stay focused. It will happen.' She winked, but he did not respond. She stared at him and then suddenly leaned forward to kiss him on the cheek. She looked deeply into his eyes, smiled sweetly and explained kindly. 'But if it doesn't work out that way for you, you can always have me.'

Rose then brushed his beard with her hand, stood up, turned and walked out of the building without saying another word.

Zeus never saw or thought of either Elixia, or Marina, ever again, so for all accounts they never existed.

Also, he never visited the woman he named Rose in person, but he did sometimes think of her, and he always had a good notion of what she was doing. He never once regretted the missed opportunity to have sex with her, but on occasion, when his memory of her was triggered by a random event, he would recount her words, quietly appreciate her simple wisdom, and enjoy a private smile.

***

For several days, Zeus spent his time relaxing. For a while he even considered returning to Mount Olympus and doing some "King of the Gods" duties. But there was no council of the gods meeting planned for the immediate future and he knew that his staff would somehow find him if anything urgent needed his attention. In his case, no news was good news.

He methodically paced the footpaths of several human settlements, but none of the women he saw or spoke with caught his interest. He was beginning to feel that he would spend the rest of his long immortal life, as a lonely old man.

Zeus admitted to himself that he was feeling frustrated with the process of finding the woman of his dreams. He was beginning to worry that he might never meet her. He pondered the solution, and had an idea that he might make an announcement. Zeus, king of the gods was seeking the perfect woman to become his wife. Please apply, with all relevant details, care of his offices in Mount Olympus. He next thought of the screening process. Intimacy would naturally feature as part of the selection process, as it would be an important part of his wife's marital duties. He smiled at the thought of a long queue of willing nubile applicants. In his imagination, many were even undressing so as to impress him. He sighed. It was good to be the king.

He morphed into his eagle form and leapt into the skies once more. It was a calm sunny day and perfect flying weather.

It was then that he flew over a Phoenician merchant sailing ship that was moored in a bay that formed a natural safe harbour. The ship was low in the water and it appeared to be laden with cargo that was covered with waterproof tarpaulins. Zeus could not workout if the merchants were inbounded, or outbound. He concluded that they were conducting business with the local Greek traders. Several smaller boats had been used to row the landing party to shore, and these were now hauled out of the water and were positioned on the pebble strewn beach.

Zeus knew that the Phoenicians were a seafaring culture. There range and influence were considerable across all Mediterranean cultures and kingdoms. They were highly regarded as traders, shipwrights, sculptors, and inventors. They had advanced agricultural techniques and were able to export surplus food stocks to other regions. Their major drawback was that the Phoenicians did not worship the Greek Gods and Goddesses, but had their own supreme god they call El. His son was known as Ba'al, and he was a powerful thunder god.

Zeus then decided that Phoenicians might not know much about Zeus, Kings of the Gods and this might be helpful when meeting these people. He decided to land and find out more about them.

***

A tent had been erected on a grassy field close to the shore, and Zeus spied a group of people that were resting on colourful blankets that were laid out on the grass. Remnants of food and wine were evident on crockery and goblets that they had used for a luncheon. The ocean water was calm and the sun was shining through clear skies bathing the Phoenicians with the warmth of a magnificent spring day. Some of the oarsmen were bathing and swimming carefree in the warm waters. Zeus slowly descended and found a tree that afforded him a suitable perch overlooking the idyllic scene.

The captain of the merchant vessel and his men began organising the replenishment of fresh water stocks from a nearby stream that flowed into the bay. They bucketed water into barrels, making several trips into the stream where it flowed fastest, as they were seeking out the clearest water. The women however, were relaxing, admiring the flowers, bird life, and butterflies that lived on the field. They seemed naively delighted by each new discovery, as if these plants and birds were new to them. As the women frolicked in the natural splendour, Zeus heard their banter, laughter, and giggling, and he smiled at their happiness. He looked for guards, but did not see any, and it seemed that the crew were unarmed, which for some reason this both pleased and relaxed him. He was totally captivated by their innocence and their oneness with the moment. Zeus morphed once more into his human form, but he remained seated within the confines of the tree, so that he was able to observe these people unobtrusively. Their activities appeared well practiced, and Zeus concluded that this captain had anchored here, in this bay many times before.

One woman stood out from the others, and she immediately intrigued him. Her beauty was breathtaking. Her flawless skin was a light-brown complexion, and her hair was shiny and jet black, and it was tied back in an elaborate ponytail, which exposed her long unblemished neck. Her eyes were so dark brown that they seemed black and her nose and ears were well shaped, and were in the correct proportion to the rest of her face. Her figure was impeccable for her smallish frame, yet her confident posture made her seem tall. Her white dress was clean and in good order, but modest in its design and not quite suited for traveling by sea. The fabric shimmered in the sunlight, and it contoured her body brilliantly. He could easily imagine her magnificence beneath her clothing. He saw some jewellery on her wrists, and they were also being worn by the other women. That was not normal for travelers, as the absence of such refinement discouraged strangers who might otherwise have criminal intent. He thought they must be very confident, or they were inexperienced.

Zeus refocused on the main woman. As he watched her, he noted that she walked with grace; her exposed calves appeared strong and were beautifully shaped. She laughed divinely, and smiled constantly as she radiated her happiness.

The other women excitedly ran up to her, revealing each new discovery they had made with childlike enthusiasm, and she received each gift with a natural regal grace. Zeus began to think that these other women might be her handmaidens. Clearly, she was a woman of high standing, and in this way, she had captured Zeus's interest as a potential candidate. He felt good and was now determined that he would meet this Phoenician beauty. Zeus drew in a deep breath as his heart raced. He then realised he was smitten with her, and he instantly became excited about the prospect of finally finding true love. He felt oddly optimistic, and his smile revealed a man brimming with anticipation. Zeus carefully descended from the tree, brushed himself off, and instantly dressed himself in modern human clothing, trying to appear as a merchant of high breeding. He then walked confidently toward the group intending to meet and hopefully seduce her. He imagined that she had a trusting and loving soul, and that she would eagerly reciprocate his advances.

He was unarmed as he wanted to give a peaceful and welcoming impression to the group of traders visiting Greece's shores. He wanted to appear as a business man who was seeking to make friends, whilst seeking out opportunities for trade and mutual profit. As he drew nearer to them, he felt uncharacteristically nervous, and when he realised his disposition, he chuckled to himself, and this relaxed him momentarily.

He passed some immature flowers in the field as he walked toward her and decided they would make a satisfactory introductory gift. As he carefully harvested them, he decided they would make a better impression if they were in full bloom, so he waved his hand over them and they quickly blossomed. Zeus told himself that this was not trickery as he had only hastened how the plant would have grown anyway. He walked closer to the group.

'Halt!' The command was shouted out toward him and Zeus stopped and watched two men walk briskly toward him. He showed them his best smile and held up the flowers.

As they drew nearer, Zeus explained. 'I wanted to give these to that woman,' he said indicating the woman of his interest.

'How do you know the princess?' the taller of the two men demanded. These were merchant sailors and not warriors, but they were naturally protective of the women in their company.

'The princess normally has a protective contingent, does she not?' Zeus wanted to appear to be familiar with the woman and her routines. He wanted to relax these two men so that they would not alert the others. He did not want this introduction to escalate the wrong way.

The other man explained, 'The princess prefers to travel incognito.' Zeus did his best not to smile at this accidental revelation.

'May I present these flowers to her highness? I feel foolish holding them before you. People might get the wrong impression about us,' Zeus suggested politely. Both men blushed and seemed uncomfortable.

'I will ask,' the taller man replied. He was about to turn to go ask the princess when he changed direction. 'Who should I say is asking to meet with her?'

'My name is Zeus, and I am a humble merchant who would like to pay his respects to the princess.'

'Did you meet with her while we were berthed at the trading port?' he queried.

'It was only for the briefest of moments, she may not even remember me,' Zeus lied, but he hoped some familiarity would help his cause.

The man walked off and the other stood still trying to relax, but unsure off what to say. Zeus avoided conversation with him and was watching the progress of the messenger. He thought he saw her nod her consent, and watched them as they both turned to walk toward him. He smiled generously at the other man who smiled and nodded his pleasure at the outcome.

As the woman drew nearer, she indicated her dismissal of the two men, who bowed respectfully and headed back to the tents.

'I am sorry, but I do not recall making your acquaintance. Who are you, kind sir?' she asked sweetly, without fear or concern.

Zeus's heart melted as her voice was delightful and wonderfully matched her beauty. 'I… am your humble servant, and the bearer of these flowers with the modest hope that they will intrigue you enough to have conversation with me.' He proffered the gift and she accepted them with a bewildered smile. These same flowers were all about them as the field was covered in a recent bloom.

'We could start with introductions,' the woman suggested inviting him to do so.

'My name is Zeus…' he began, but she cut him off with her laughter.

'You were named after the king of the Greek Gods! Your parents were quite presumptuous,' she concluded. 'You must have been teased a lot as a child?'

Zeus had had an unusual childhood, but being teased had not featured in it. He decided he would play along with the way this meeting was progressing. It was possible that his being a god might confuse or even frighten her, and he did not want to let that happen.

'I have been compared to him on a few occasions…' but her laughter cut him off again. He waited patiently hoping that this levity would help him gain her trust.

'My man thought we had met you before, when we were at the markets, but I am certain I would have remembered you.' She looked quizzically at him. She did not seem apprehensive or concerned. 'I gather you are one of the traders my men dealt with?'

Zeus tried to appear sad. 'Yet, I was unsuccessful,' Zeus said softly whilst bowing, pretending to show a failing, whilst trying desperately to appear confident. 'You see my quality is highly-rated and my prices match, and we were unable to strike a deal.'

The woman nodded her understanding. "This trip was to deliver a consignment of carpets and assorted floor coverings. For the return journey we purchased products that are suitable to be sold in our home markets. Quality has never been the major concern. So, you thought to come here to trade with us here. You can see our ship is already loaded to the hilt.' She pointed to the cargo vessel in the bay. What do you trade in?'

Zeus decided that using the Persian carpet line was a wasted effort. He switched to something he knew more about. 'I deal in weapons.'

'We are already well equipped and as we are not at war with anyone, so we probably won't need to buy anything from you,' she explained but she did not appear either happy, or sad, about disappointing his business plans. Merchants were supposed to take it as it comes.

Zeus was staring at the sailing ship when he suddenly had an inspiration. 'I also sell inflatable clothing for people to wear when they are out to sea. It assists buoyancy when they fall into the water.'

Her eyes widened. 'That could be interesting.' She smiled at him. 'Perhaps we can set up a meeting for our next buying trip in twenty-eight days' time.'

'I had hoped to become better acquainted with you before then,' Zeus declared his intentions.

She smiled invitingly. 'I believe I would like that.'

Zeus suddenly became aware of his dilemma. As he had said that he had tried to do business with these people at the markets, then it should be obvious that he knew the name of the woman he came to meet. But he did not, and his plans would be shattered if he asked.

He was rescued by one of the hand maidens who raced up to them and gave a brief curtsy before saying... 'Europa, we have prepared chairs, food and refreshments for you and your guest,' the young woman explained and was smiling as she pointed toward the arrangements.

'Excellent,' Europa replied and clapped her hands in her appreciation to the young woman. She then turned toward Zeus indicating her invitation for him to join her on the arranged seating.

As they walked to the chairs and food and drink, Zeus's mind was racing. Europa was a beautiful name and she was a princess. Did not all princesses want to become a queen when they grew up? He was searching for a queen, and she would fit perfectly into his plans.

'Zeus,' Europa said interrupting his thoughts. 'Would you like some food, or perhaps wine? She was personally offering both of these to him. Her handmaidens had now discreetly hidden themselves out of view.

Zeus realised he was famished, but remembered to accept humbly and take only small portions as was polite custom. 'Europa is a beautiful name, and you are the first that I have ever met that has it.'

'It means far seeing, or wide seeing. My parents planned that I should grow up an enlightened woman, and believed that I should have a name that reflects their aspirations for me. I am a modern woman.' She paused studying his face to see if he understood and accepted this notion, but Zeus said and did nothing. 'Perhaps you could tell me the real reason why you are here?' Europa invited. She neither smiled nor appeared concerned.

Zeus almost blushed, and he then decided to be forthright. He would throw caution into the wind and see where it landed. 'I grow weary of living the life of a bachelor. I am hoping to find the perfect woman with a view to achieving true love resulting in everlasting marriage.'

Europa burst into laughter once more. Zeus's face blushed a bright crimson red. His overtures of love and lust to other woman had never earned him this response before. It was true he was now trying to do so as a mere mortal, but he still had hoped his magnificence would have at least tempted her. If this was how human women responded to their men, then Zeus was grateful to be a god.

'Oh, you poor thing,' she said seemingly sorry that she had embarrassed him. 'Look!' she exclaimed, trying to sound perky. Let us get to know each other a little first, perhaps share some stories about ourselves, and learn some details about each other, before we plan our wedding?'

Zeus drew in a deep breath but chose to say nothing.

Europa took his silence as acquiescence, as so she relaxed into her seat, and was about to speak when she looked about puzzled. She then stood and called to the captain. 'We must leave soon.'

The captain agreed nodding at her and her guest. 'I've instructed the men to strike the tents and reload the ship. We'll set sail as soon as you are ready.'

Europa sat down and turned to Zeus. 'I am sorry but we do not have much time. It is important that we return to Phoenicia by tomorrow morning. We will sail through the night.'

Zeus nodded his understanding and tried hard not to show his disappointment. He too had noticed the tide. He could delay it, but that might be obvious.

She turned to him and leaned forward. 'Okay, I will start,' Europa decided. 'It will be like a speed date without any of those complicated expectations.' Europa laughed and Zeus found himself liking this woman enormously.

'My parents are Agenor and Telephassa and they are King and Queen of Phoenicia. My brothers and I are close, but not too close.' Zeus understood what she implied. Formal relationships between royal siblings were common to protect the family heritage and bloodlines. 'My mother is Phoenician, and we all live in the city of Tyre and we are direct descendants of that tribe. I can also speak in the Punic dialect with my family, though we tend to speak Greek more often than our own language. Fortunately for you and for our date today, I am unwed, however, I am promised to marry Asterion, the future King of Crete, but as yet no wedding date has been agreed upon.'

'Do you love him?' Zeus asked dreading her response.

'I've never met him,' she replied dourly. 'I will honour my parent's agreement to the best of my ability. Hopefully, love will follow...' she said letting her words hang heavily. Then she perked up. 'Unless of course, I meet the man of my dreams, who excites my wildest passions, and can promise me a grander life. One who can do so without any recriminations from my parents, Asterion, or the Phoenician people!' she said studying Zeus face wide eyed for his reaction.

Zeus was now besotted with her. Europa's words made his heart leap with joy, but at the same time he was wary of being mocked and being punished with her laughter. He wanted to avoid falling into a female trap by mistaking her charm as overtures. He simply grinned like a happy idiot, too scared to verbally react to this plea to rescue her.

'I believe I would make Asterion a good wife, and that I would be a worthy queen. I love children and hope to give birth to many babies of my own. I can read and write and have scribed numerous stories capturing the history of my peoples. I am proud to be African, but I accept that my destiny lies with my future husband in Crete.' She looked to him for his reaction but the noises of the nearby men dismantling the tents, and her hand maidens packing away the blankets and food baskets distracted her, thus giving Zeus time to ponder.

He now doubted that a declaration that he was Zeus, king of the gods, and the most powerful force in all the lands was the right thing to do? If he stuck with the story of being a trader in quality goods then he may be an inadequate suitor for her highness. But in revealing that he was a powerful god, he would be exposing his earlier lie. She wanted love and babies and he could certainly give her plenty of those, but would she laugh at him if he said he was more than just a merchant.

'Quickly Zeus, tell me enough about yourself so that I will agree to meet with you once more, here in twenty-eight days' time,' Europa challenged.

'I am healthy, strong, respected, and wealthy beyond comparison. I am loyal, faithful, and loving.' He paused watching her getting up and preparing to leave him. He was beginning to feel desperate. 'In four weeks', when you return, I will present you with a token of love that will outlast and outdo any gift of love that was ever given by a man to a woman,' he said making this promise to her.

Europa stood up and smiled. 'I will accept your invitation to meet with you once again. But if the gift is jewellery, I have plenty. I also own a magnificent wardrobe. I have my own stables, and I am attended too by skilled physicians. There is little a merchant can offer that will tempt me away from my current status. I will require that your gift be symbolic of true, enduring, and eternal love. I will also need to learn a lot more about you.'

The captain and most of his crew and passengers were now on board the vessel. Two men remained on shore, and they now carried the two chairs that Europa and Zeus had just relinquished. They then waited patiently, ready to row the tender that would carry them from the shore to the ship.

'It will be so. I will be here in twenty-eight days to present such a gift to you.'

They bowed to each other and she turned and walked to the wooden tender. After she sat down and as the men heaved the craft off the beach, she waved to him and he returned her wave with equal measure. He had much to ponder. He waited until the ship hauled up the anchor and he watched the sails fill with the wind as the vessel turned toward the open sea. He then changed once more into his eagle form, and took to the skies to return home to Mount Olympus.

***

One of Europa's hand maidens approached her mistress. 'He seemed nice.'

Europa sighed heavily. She nodded to the woman. 'I think we should only talk about Zeus in terms of the inventory that he is offering to sell us.'

The woman said nothing, but Europa understood the silence.

Europa drew in a deep breath and let out a heavy sigh. 'Yes, okay, he is handsome and well-spoken, and he is kind of cute,' she capitulated.

'Kind of cute! The way you were gushing over him, I thought you were going to rip his clothes off and have your way with him.'

'I would never,' Europa frowned as she started to protest. Then she realised that the woman was only teasing. 'I will admit that the thought of bedding him did have some appeal.'

'One last fling before your wedding day?'

Europa did not confirm the possibility, but she did not rule it out either.

***

When Zeus arrived at his Mount Olympus palace, he was inundated with numerous, and mostly annoying duties that he needed to deal with. His administrative staff were a good team, and they did well to manage the mundane and mostly clerical duties imposed on them. They were also experienced enough to leave the more delicate decisions to the boss. He was tactful and pleasing with most plaintiff's when he dealt with minor disputes between deities, by quickly choosing to be fair with outcomes. Later, his senior aide told him that Prometheus was ready to present his prototypes of the new Cow and

Bull to him, and that Zeus was invited to his home to inspect these new beasts.

Zeus decided he was tired, and that he would rest first and then deal with Prometheus later. He and his new farm animals would wait. After drinking several cups of wine, and eating a modest meal of mutton and vegetables, Zeus laid back in his bed pondering the gift he would give to Europa without resorting to using trickery or any of his many powers. The gift must seem God worthy, but be believable that it was delivered into her hand by a humble mortal. After a while he had formed a notion of two things that he could gift to her. His first idea related to the naming of a spectacular moon after her, in perpetual honour. It was one of the moons that circled an enormous planet that he had named after himself, despite Helios' claim that it was named after his son, Phaethon. He had already used this gift to reward the Cretan nymph Adrastea, for her devotion and care that she gave him when he was a just an infant. It seemed that his planet had ample moons for him to use in this manner.

But it was his second idea that really appealed to him. He decided to gift her the first ever bull. He believed that she would be extremely impressed to be the first human to ever have such a beast. Zeus was now able to rest comfortably, satisfied that these gifts had sufficient potential to win her heart. He was now thinking loving thoughts about Europa, and the future happiness that they would enjoy together. Slowly, Zeus drifted off into a deep sleep. Later, a servant came to clear the dishes, but he stopped when he realised that the boss was sleeping. He was delighted when he also noticed that the boss was smiling.

***

The following morning when Zeus awoke, he thought more about his plans. He suddenly realized that he had better scrutinize this bull.

If it were a hideous creature, or too fierce, it may have the opposite effect when he presented it to Europa. He dressed and rushed out from his palace and hastily journeyed to Prometheus's residence to inspect these new animals.

When he arrived, he found both the Cow and the Bull in a barn contentedly munching their way through a pile of hay. Both beasts lifted their heads and looked impassively at him. Neither were alarmed at Zeus's presence. They shifted their immense weight and resumed eating. Zeus thought they were magnificent. He found Prometheus asleep in his bed chamber and did not hesitate to wake him. 'I am pleased and delighted with these new beasts, Prometheus, well done.'

Prometheus quickly dressed and they headed for the barn. 'I waited up for you,' he gently admonished his king.

'Sorry, but urgent affairs of state took all my attention,' Zeus replied by way of an explanation of why he had not visited him sooner. Zeus had never really liked Prometheus, and never totally trusted him because he was a Titan. But he had value, and his creations were mostly impressive and useful. It was his persistent benevolence towards humans that was most annoying, and the two often clashed. They had differing opinions as to how to treat humans, and how to manage their growth and development as a society of people. Zeus appreciated the value of fear and awe that the humans held for their gods and goddesses. Prometheus however, wanted to encourage human independence from Mount Olympian rule. Zeus believed that he and Prometheus would clash heavily one day, and that it would be Prometheus that would suffer for it.

Prometheus, as the God of foresight, also knew that this would happen, but for now he capitulated gracefully. Zeus was the most powerful of all the gods, but he was often unreasonable and stubborn.

Prometheus already knew that one day he would be punished by Zeus, and that his sentence would be arduous and filled with suffering.

For now, they stood together calmly and cooperatively, as they examined the docile beasts. 'Does their meat taste good?' Zeus asked, but Prometheus's expression was such that they did, and that this fact should have been a forgone conclusion.

'The meat tastes much better when it is cooked. My aides preferred the meat cooked until it is almost blackened, and they seemed to get much delight from it. Personally, I thought they had overdone it, so I tasted my slice while the meat was still moist and succulent. The juices are what made it desirable to me, while the longer cook portions seemed too dried out. I guess it will become a matter of personal preference.'

They studied each other thoughtfully. 'I would like to try some of this meat,' Zeus ordered.

Prometheus left Zeus to gaze at the bull and his cow whilst he arranged for more of the meat from a previously butchered cow to be cooked. He instructed his aides to remove the meat from the hot plate at various times so that some still showed it bloody redness right through to it being fully cooked. In that way, Zeus could try each for himself. After some time, the meal was ready and so Zeus worked his way through each portion with the air of a professional judge of cooked meats. He made a play of it, scrutinising the nuances of the rare, medium, and fully cooked meat offerings. He smiled and was delighted with all the offerings. 'I agree with you, Prometheus.' He then stepped closer to the Titan. 'The meat that has a middle layer of pinkness is also my preferred result. I agree with you that this will develop into a range of personal preferences. I hereby approve this animal for introduction into both the Gods and the human population.'

Prometheus bowed gracefully, pleased with Zeus's determination and pronouncement. His smile faded as Zeus continued with his judgement.

'However, until these beasts can increase in their numbers, I am reserving the choicest cuts of meats for exclusive consumption by the gods and goddesses here at Mount Olympus. I want you to prepare me two platters, one reserved for the gods and the other for the humans. This is how it will be, Prometheus. See to it.'

Zeus left the Titan to the task. He knew that he had upset him, but Prometheus often exceeded his position, and regularly needed to be reminded of his place.

***

Later that day, Zeus received a message from Prometheus that the division of the new meat was completed. He was invited to visit and give his approval of the allocation of meat, and so Zeus set off to Prometheus's residence once more. When he arrived, Prometheus presented him with two open sacks, and then invited Zeus to select the sack that would become the meat exclusively for the gods. The other sack would end up being the second-grade cuts of meat for the humans to cook and eat. The first sack had all the choicest cuts of meat in it, but Prometheus had laid the beasts stomach on top of the meat, making it appear unappetising. The second sack contained the offal and bones but they were hidden from view by a rich layer of prime beefy meat.

Zeus studied the two sacks and then examined Prometheus. He sensed the trickery, but decided that this was now his opportunity to catch Prometheus red handed as the blood from the meat still stained his hands.

'I choose this one.' Zeus said pointing to the sack containing the bones and the offal. Prometheus couldn't help himself and smiled. Zeus then reached forward and tipped out the contents of the sack that had the choice cuts and the cow's stomach. As the good meat spilled out, Zeus turned to Prometheus and spoke harshly. 'You have deceived me! The humans may consume this meat, but they can only eat it raw. No fire, or heat, will be allowed to be used in its preparation.'

'But Zeus, that is unfair. Raw meat is unworthy of humans. I protest. Please allow them to cook this meat.' Prometheus was being forceful with his god king and hoped that this would not develop into something he would regret, although he already knew that he would.

'They can make what they like from its milk,' Zeus said pointing to the milk udder under the cow.

'But Zeus, surely you would not make them eat it raw!' Prometheus protested.

'And they can thank you for that decree!' Zeus bellowed. 'If you persist with badgering me, I will remove fire from all human activities.' The king stared harshly at the Titan. He then relaxed a little. 'For now, they will only be allowed to eat raw cow.'

As Zeus's determination hung heavily in the air, Prometheus bowed in acquiescence, whilst he watched his lordship leave to return to his palace.

***

For the next four weeks Prometheus set about increasing the numbers of Cows and Bulls by quickly replicating them from the approved prototypes. He set about distributing them among the human tribes that had homes within a reasonable proximity to Mount Olympus.

Prometheus showed humans how to harvest the milk from the cows. The females needed to first birth a calf in order to produce the milk, and the bulls seemed willing to participate in this process. The humans were confused and disappointed as to why they could never butcher the animal, as Prometheus had forbidden it as a condition of his gift of the cow's and the bulls to them. Soon, human pressure mounted, and they demanded to eat the meat they raised. So, Prometheus finally capitulated and decided that he would once again disobey Zeus, and gift them the fire they would use to cook the meat. He symbolically smuggled a glowing ember of fire within a stalk of a fennel plant out of Mount Olympus, and he shared it with the humans, telling them that they must cook their beef in secrecy.

When Zeus spied cooking fires from Mount Olympus, he immediately investigated and revealed Prometheus's disobedience. He pretended to be shocked and angry. The humans were now fearful and they offered animal sacrifices to appease the king of the gods. Zeus had achieved his goal in humbling the humans. So, he gracefully capitulated, and granted them his approval to cook the meat. They rejoiced his benevolence, and celebrated the cooking of the meat in his honour. Many feasts were held praising Zeus, reaffirming their loyalty and deference toward him.

Secretly however, Zeus was pleased that he now had the reason to formally punish the Titan. He summonsed Prometheus, charged him with disobedience, and then had him secured. He later imprisoned Prometheus by using superior quality adamantine chains to fasten him to a large rock, high up in the Caucasus Mountains.

Zeus then changed into his eagle form and flew away. As he did, he summoned another eagle who was similar in size and power to him. The bird's name was Aquila and Zeus arranged for Aquila to visit Prometheus each day to rip out, and eat the Titan's liver. He knew that as an immortal, Prometheus's would grow a new liver, and that his wound would heal each day. It was in this way that Prometheus's torment would last for an eternity.

Much later, Prometheus would finally be freed by Herakles while he was completing his ten labours.

***

In the days leading up to Zeus's rendezvous with Europa, Zeus practiced changing himself into a resplendent white Bull. Zeus preferred to travel great distances morphed in his eagle form, but he was so impressed with Prometheus's animal design that he wanted to master morphing into the bulls' form also. Being the king of the gods meant that when Zeus was in his bull form that his horns were slightly larger and pointier than the Prometheus prototype. Also, Zeus decided to have the brightest and whitest hide to show-off how clean he was. He had a muscular body befitting the king of the gods. Zeus gazed at his bovine reflection. He enlarged his brown eyes, and increased the length of his eye lashes. He reduced the length of the snout and lengthened the ears. Zeus was pleased to admit to himself that his version of the bull was the cutest he had ever seen, and he was exceedingly confident that even in this form, he would win the love and devotion of the beautiful, Europa.

***

On the twenty-eighth day since last seeing Europa, Zeus told his staff that he would be absent from Mount Olympus for some time. He remembered to remind them that he had every confidence in their ability, and they dutifully pretended to be appreciative of his praise. They had heard it all before, and they all knew that the important work they did for the immortals of Mount Olympus, would continue unaffected by their boss's departure.

Zeus morphed and flew directly to the bay where he hoped the merchant ship would be anchored for his arranged reunion with Europa. He was excited when he saw that it was there. He circled the skies looking down on the serenity of the ship at anchor, and he spotted the Phoenicians relaxing on blankets, eating foods, and drinking wine, and enjoying the fresh water from the stream. He noted that Europa was looking out toward the forest, and he hoped that she was eagerly waiting for him to arrive.

He landed in the same tree as before and instantly morphed into his Zeus form. He was wearing similar clothing to what he had worn the earlier time they met, trying to maintain the impression that he was a successful merchant. With long confident strides, he walked out of the forest and once more approached the group of people. This time he was unchallenged by the men, and he watched Europa rise from her chair to walk out to greet him.

Europa's companions also stood up, but To Zeus's surprise they walked away, leaving Zeus completely alone with their mistress.

'Zeus, you are welcome,' Europa greeted him with a smile and modest curtsy.

'Europa, your pleasure at seeing me, lifts my heart and makes my spirits soar,' he said smiling with his most endearing charm and then he performed an exaggerated bow.

She laughed and relaxed into a smile. Her smile faded and her face changed into one of concern. Her eyes narrowed as she stared at him. 'When we were in town, my men and I sought you out. No-one has heard of Zeus the trader. Your name is infrequently used due to Zeus being the name of the king of all the Greek gods. They say many avoid using his name for their children, as it may bring about his displeasure and wrath.'

'Oh,' Zeus paused and reflected. 'I am sure he is not all that bad. He might even think of it as a compliment,' Zeus defended.

'He has a ferocious temper you know. I have never personally met him, but I believe that it is true that he does,' Europa admitted with a frown as she examined his face.

Zeus said nothing. He stoically maintained his calm and poise.

'But something I have recently learned, is that the great God Zeus is also seeking love and romance, and that he too is on the prowl for a wife.' She stepped up closer to him. 'Just like you are.'

'An odd coincidence,' Zeus replied with concern, obviously taken a bit back by this revelation. This encounter was not going the way he had hoped.

'Let us assume for a moment, that you are not Zeus the Greek merchant specialising in top quality trade goods, but that you are actually Zeus, the magnificent God of all the Greek Gods and Goddesses, and that you are now actively seducing me toward a permanent relationship.'

Both Zeus's would be lucky to have your love and devotion,' Zeus said meekly, not sure which way this interchange was heading.

'What gifts would Zeus the merchant offer to me, to win my favours? His undying love, his perpetual romance, or would it be common jewels, clothes, or gold?'

'All that, and more,' Zeus conceded.

'So, what gift would Zeus the God give me? It would need to be far more impressive than mere clothing or valuables. How would a god such as Zeus gift me his undying love and perpetual romance with me being a lowly mortal?'

'As a god I would bestow the gift of immortality. In that way you would enjoy his love and protection for all time. As a god I would bestow the gift of acquisition, so that anything you wanted would be yours. Although, I confess that the novelty of that power will soon diminish in value. One gift I hoped would impress you, was the gift of a moon.' He paused to gauge her reaction.

'Selene?' Europa was confused.

'No, not Selene.' Zeus smiled at the thought explaining that to Selene. As Earth's Moon goddess she would not approve. 'The moon I refer to rotates about the giant planet that shares my name. It is known by all Greeks as Zeus, and it has a moon keeping it perpetual company. As a god I would name that moon "Europa" in your honour.'

Europa studied Zeus's face. He looked and sounded sincere. She could not contain herself and burst into laughter. When she relaxed, she responded. 'Well, Zeus the God. That is a truly magnificent gift which I appreciatively accept. But that gift seems so far away, and I cannot see it, or use it for any purpose. Truly, everyone will learn that it is named in my honour, and so my name will endure for many millennia. But my moon is lonely, and remote, and so very cold in the far reaches of space, and the thought of it all alone gives me mixed emotions. I am elated that it is mine, but I am sad for its disposition,' Europa said sounding genuinely conflicted.

Zeus's heart melted. 'Do you have a favoured relative that I could honour with a different moon to keep your moon company?'

Europa seemed thoughtful. 'Do you know my great-great grand-mother, Io?'

Zeus shook his head. He had no memory of her. He was not surprised as there were so many names, people, places, gods, and goddesses to remember. 'I could consult my palace staff and enquire after her?' he offered.

'So, you own a palace, and you have staff? Now you do sound much more like Zeus the god, and much less like Zeus the humble merchant,' she accused as she examined him. 'Do you confess?'

A lie never works with women. He could not recall a time when any deceit leveled at a female had survived once the truth was discovered. 'I do. I am he.'

'If you sanction it, my great-great grandmother's moon could look after my moon as it circled your mighty planet.'

'Then it will be so. A moon will forever be named, Io,' Zeus replied.

'So, Zeus the god wants to make me his wife,' she said as she walked a circle around him summarising their situation. 'He wants to offer me his undying love and he will romance me, and keep me happy. He wants to make me immortal, and grant me divine powers.' She turned to face him as she examined his face, but he said and did nothing.

'These moons are too far away to make an effective gift. I am not impressed. What else have you got for me?'

Zeus thought quickly. She was impressed with something being named in her honour, but the problem was that it was too remote, too far away. His gift was not tangible enough. An idea was mulling in his mind, and he spoke forming the words as he uttered them. 'Your home is Phoenicia. South of here, across the sea is a region widely known as Africa. You travel the African coastline to conduct your trade with the numerous kingdoms that reside there,'

Europa nodded he agreement and understanding.

Zues continued. 'We also know of Asia, and that it has many nations thriving within its boundaries. Here, we are in Greece. This nation is only one of many nations whose population numbers keep growing with many more people. It still has no common name, but it is within my power to name everything north and west of here, all the way to the furthest oceans, and I now choose to do so in your honour. It shall be forever named, Europa!'

Europa was stunned. To have all the combined nations that were north and west of Greece named Europa after her, was indeed a great honour. She hoped that all these people would accept the use of her name, and that she would be remembered forever. Slowly she nodded her head, 'I embrace your kindness, and I am deeply humbled by your gesture,' she blurted.

Zeus was both relieved and elated. Why had he not thought of this gift earlier. 'So, Europa, will you accept me as your lover and future husband?' Zeus thought this was the best time to capitalise on her gratitude.

'Zeus, the god.' She reached up and touched his face with one hand. 'Please grant me the time to properly consider the consequences of accepting your proposal. Your gift of a moon surrounding your planet and the naming of all these lands in my honour, are truly amazing gifts. Your offer to love me and bestow me with immortality is such a big step for me, please, give me some time to think on this, as I wish to ponder all the repercussions.'

'But...' Zeus began to protest.

She held up her hand and Zeus recognised the sign. He conceded that a woman worth having is a woman that you do not rush into making a decision. He nodded his resigned capitulation. She continued explaining. 'Please come back tomorrow and I will share with you some food, some wine, and my decision. Please be prepared to hear bad news, as I am betrothed to another, and my betrayal of him will go down abysmally with my family.'

'Would becoming the Queen of all the Gods and Goddesses of Mount Olympus, remove that issue?

'You have not met my father.' Europa sighed.

Zeus stared at her. He capitulated, bowed, turned, and walked away from her. Once in the trees he morphed into his eagle form and flew directly to Mount Olympus.

***

The following day he flew back to the bay where the ship was anchored, and he was relieved to see that it was still there. He landed, morphed, and set off to discover his fate with his chosen intended.

Europa spied him entering the field from his usual entry point. She was curious about his mode of transport, but accepted that it would be godlike, and therefore beyond her mortal understanding. Zeus strode confidently toward her and stopped, opening his arms, and he was grinning happily. His manner dissolved when she did not rush into his arms as he had hoped.

'Have I not done enough to impress you?' Zeus asked gently.

'I still need more time,' she replied looking down at her feet. Her head lifted. 'I hardly know you beyond your reputation. I do know that that is insufficient, as there are so many stories about you that they all cannot be true…' she said as her voice trailed off.

'They might,' Zeus confessed. 'I will admit, I've done some questionable things…' his voice also trailing off.

They examined each other, neither was confident enough to speak. 'Please understand,' Zeus finally blurted. 'A gift of true love from you, as the woman who would become my wife, will change me. I will settle down, and we will share a life of true love, happiness, and together we will start and raise our family.'

'You already have many children,' Europa chided him.

'I have fathered a few,' Zeus conceded. 'But I have never raised them as a family. None of my children have ever lived with me. I never made a home for their mother or the children we conceived. I would happily with you. I would share my palace on Mount Olympus with you and only you. I will openly admit my palace needs a woman's touch, but it would be your home also, and you would change it to suit you.' Zeus realised he was now sounding like a man who was pleading, and so he abruptly stopped.

Europa smiled and reached out and stroked his bearded face. She reached forward and gently kissed him on the lips. She withdrew and smiled up at him. She drew in a deep breath and spoke gently. 'You poor boy, you are struck down with love sickness. In truth, I am honoured. I find myself drawn to you, and to your proposal. But I am also conflicted as I am betrothed to Asterion, the King of Crete, and my parents have made a commitment to him that I have already promised to keep.'

Zeus was confused. He was resolved to accept her decision without consequences, recriminations, or trickery. He appealed to her as humbly as any man can do to a woman, when he discovers himself forlorn in unrequited love. He drew in a deep breath. 'I had hoped that by being married to the king of all of the gods, that you would impress them even more.'

She smiled, nodded, and spoke softly. 'I will ask them.'

They stood staring at each other, uncertain of what to do or say. Their awkward silence was interrupted by the captain who shouted to her that the ship would be ready to sail in one hour. They both examined the vessel, and it appeared to be ready to leave at a moment's notice. They smiled knowing the captain was being polite.

Europa smiled again and then spoke reassuringly. 'Meet me here again. In twenty-eight days, and I will give you, my answer.'

Zeus wanted to object and utter his disappointment at the eternal wait, but he resisted. He also wanted to leap for joy as she had given him some hope, but he stoically resisted. He wanted to weep in dire misery at the thought of her ultimate rejection, but again, he resisted. So, Zeus said nothing, and he simply nodded his acceptance of decision.

Europa reached up and lightly kissed him on the lips once more, and then left him standing alone in the field. She quickly returned to the others on the pebble beach, and they boarded the small tender. He watched the crew propel the craft into the gentle ocean water, and then they rowed her to the merchant ship. He watched them climb aboard, haul up the tender, weigh anchor, and hoist the sails. He next watched the wind fill those sails, and he clearly heard the captain give the orders to make for sea. He sat on a fallen tree and watched the departing vessel until it reached the horizon.

Zeus sighed, took in another deep breath, morphed once more into his eagle form, flapped his wings, and took to the skies once more. He decided he needed to meet with his brother, Poseidon.

***

Zeus called out to his brother. Communication between them was often problematic. Sometimes an impulsive invitation was met with a quick response, but only if Poseidon was not otherwise occupied. Formal requests were often ignored, in particular if they involved him being at meetings of the high council. If he were distracted, his older brother would just ignore him. When in the throes of a romantic liaison, or some trivial pursuit, then Poseidon was all about Poseidon. Zeus knew that being the king of gods and goddesses earned him scant respect from his siblings. None of them feared him, and once when he did confront them about it, they shrugged him off and reminded him that he too was egocentric, that it was a family trait, and that he should just deal with it. They told him to just get on with it and do whatever it was that he intended to do.

On this occasion however, Poseidon responded instantly, and he agreed to meet him once more at their favourite rendezvous place at the eatery by the sea. They arrived at the same time. On entering the premises, and to the owner's dismay, his other patrons hastily exited the premises. The brothers were instantly recognisable, and it was common knowledge that disputes between them could result in the destruction of furniture, cause collateral human injuries, and even sometimes bring about the inadvertent death of innocent bystanders.

The proprietor hoped they were in a good mood, and that they would again be overly generous when compensating him for all the considerable quantities of food and wine that they would consume. He willingly agreed to let them use his establishment as their meeting place, to the exclusion of all others, as if he had any choice.

'Are you still searching for true love and your future wife?' Poseidon asked as kindly as he could. They were seated at their regular table, and they beckoned the owner for wine. Poseidon rested his beloved golden and bejewelled trident carefully against the furniture. He rarely traveled without it. Zeus stared at it without interest.

'As a matter of fact, I am not,' Zeus replied with a wry smile on his face.

'Either you have found the perfect woman but have discovered a depressing conflict about her, or you have resolved to yourself that she does not exist, and so you have given up,' Poseidon concluded with a smile.

'The first one,' Zeus agreed. 'I have not given up, but I am beginning to think I should re-start my search.'

'The perfect woman has been found! Have you seen her naked?'

'What?'

'Have you seen her naked?' Poseidon repeated.

'No, why is that relevant?'

'Beautiful bare breasts bedazzle boys beyond belief,' Poseidon explained.

'I do not understand what you mean,' Zeus was confused.

'Seeing them naked, or having sex with them clouds the brain.'

'Oh, no. Nothing like that has happened,' Zeus assured his brother.

'So, you have met the perfect woman, but she has insurmountable baggage?' Poseidon chortled. He was totally amused by his brother's love life problems.

'She is betrothed,' Zeus explained.

'That should not be an issue. You should just kill him, or... you could change him into a fish.' He suggested rationally as if speaking from experience.

'He is the King of Crete. I would lose popularity with his people if I did anything dramatic to him. Besides, Europa would know of it, and she would not approve.'

'Europa?' He chuckled. Poseidon was clearly more amused than before. 'You do realise that she is a Phoenician princess?' He grinned at his brother, delighted to be able to torment him.

'She is the most beautiful, and the most wonderful woman that I have ever met. She is smart, resourceful, witty, and at the same time innocently playful.'

'So, you have bedded her?'

Zeus appeared hurt, but he did not reply.

Poseidon bellowed in unrestrained laughter. He calmed down when the owner delivered a jug of wine and two oversized sturdy goblets. He set them down and poured. Poseidon reached for his and downed the drink in one gulp. He motioned to the man to refill the goblet and he did as he was beckoned. Zeus's goblet remained untouched.

Poseidon studied him. 'You've got it bad brother. Just copulate with her and then dump her. Get this woman out of your system.'

'She would not do it,' Zeus said dismally.

'Use trickery.'

Zeus winced. He was determined not to use deceit or any of his godly powers to win her heart. He wanted her to love him for all the right reasons. He shook his head. 'I won't do it.'

'Europa, Europa,' Poseidon said thoughtfully, smacking his lips noisily. 'Europa's mother is a delightful girl named Telephassa.'

'So, she told me.'

'Telephassa's mother is a stunning woman named Libya.'

'I have heard of her,' Zeus said and was now curious.

'You have,' he said, and then he grinned. 'From me,' Poseidon continued and nodded knowingly. 'I had my way with her. I did her good and proper and she enjoyed it a lot. And guess what, we even made a baby together.' He paused to smile in anticipation of the reveal. 'I am Telephassa's seed father. Europa is my granddaughter.'

Zeus winced and Poseidon laughed once more clearly enjoying his brother's discomfort.

The owner next delivered platters of food. Poseidon started eagerly eating from the seafood platter, but Zeus stared at the cooked beef, mutton, pork, and vegetables on the plate without appetite.

'If you marry Europa, then I will become your grandfather,' Poseidon said and grinned at him with a mouthful of food. The expression was threatening to choke him, so he swallowed hard and washed down the food with a gulp of wine. He then sniggered and smiled again. 'This account gets even better. Libya's mother is named Memphis, and she was also a lovely girl by the way.'

'So?'

'She is the daughter of the magnificent, Io.'

'Now I remember Io.' Zeus was forming a memory from long ago. 'Oddly enough, I have only just named a moon after her.'

'Did you? That is funny, because you already did that once before. You did it as a thank you for being a good girl when you had finished copulating with her. By the way, she got pregnant, and you are Memphis's seed father. So, as it works out, that because of my interlude with Libya, it makes you, my grandfather.'

Zeus was working it all out in his mind when Poseidon declared it. 'If you marry Europa, and if all our earlier relationships had become permanent ones, then in theory you would be my grandson, I would be both your grandson and your grandfather, and you would become your own great, great, grandfather!' Poseidon laughed so much that the table shook and threatened to spill the wine.

The owner looked over in concern, but there was no retribution from Zeus, and so he relaxed and continued to hover close by and to be ready to serve when needed.

Poseidon offered Zeus his brotherly advice. 'Have your way with her and move on. Wives are overrated.'

They talked some more about Europa, but made no progress. Zeus's fate lay in Europa's decision, and he was firmly resolved to wait the twenty-eight days to learn her answer.

'How did Prometheus get on with designing his cow?' Poseidon asked changing the subject.

'He did well,' Zeus replied, relieved to be talking about something else. He reached over to the uneaten steak part of the meal and picked it up showing Poseidon. 'This meat is from that beast.'

'It cannot be any good. You did not eat any of it,' Poseidon observed.

'Oh, it is good, exceptional in fact,' Zeus defended. 'I just do not seem to have an appetite.'

'Poor boy,' Poseidon teased. 'You really do have it bad.' He was referring to Zeus's doubtful marriage prospects. 'What does the finished beast look like?'

Zeus rose from his chair. 'Come outside and I will show you,' he invited.

Poseidon followed his brother outside. On their way out and despite not having consumed any of the food or wine, Zeus compensated the owner generously. As was custom between the two brothers, the inviter paid all expenses. Both knew they could leave without paying, but human devotion to them was something they were keen to maintain.

Zeus checked for observers and when he was satisfied that they were alone, he morphed into his magnificent white bull form. Poseidon gasped, clearly impressed by the animal. Zeus proudly paraded about before changing back into his godly human form.

'Is it any good for riding?' Poseidon asked.

'It was not really designed for it, but I suppose it could suit that purpose. Its speed is slow and not good for anything but short distances. I suppose it could be used for pulling heavy loads. Prometheus designed it to be easily caught, herded, and managed. I believe he planned to tame wolves and train them to assist humans with that task.'

'He did well,' Poseidon observed. 'I promised the Athenian's a beast that would be suitable for riding fast, and would have the stamina for long distances. I will ask Prometheus to assist me. I think we could remodel his design by lengthening the legs and the neck, and by narrowing the girth and its head, and that we could make it work.'

'Prometheus has seriously disobeyed me, and he is now serving an extended sentence chained to a rock,' Zeus explained casually.

'I can manage it on my own,' Poseidon did not like Prometheus much either.

Zeus pondered his brother's plans. 'I suggest you also remove the horns, or they may do the rider an injury if they fall over the front of it, if it stops suddenly. Your beast should prove popular. What will you call it?'

'The Athenian's want me to call it a "Horse."'

The brothers finally bid each other a fond farewell. Poseidon wished his brother well. 'Do not forget to invite me to the wedding,' he teased.

Poseidon returned to his watery domain, and Zeus morphed into his Eagle form, and then flew to Mount Olympus to wait it out until he could meet with Europa once more, to learn her answer.

***

Zeus returned home to Mount Olympus in time to chair the meeting of the council of gods. Attending was optional, and the constituents of the council varied according to Zeus's whims. Although Poseidon was a permanent member, he was more often absent than present, giving his brother his vote in absentia. This suited Zeus, as often it made it easier for him to exercise his own will. Athena was also a permanent member, and she too often sided with her father. She was enthusiastic, practical, and would always make worthy contributions. Her observations during the proceedings were always respected. Athena often clashed with Poseidon, who tended to be flippant about human needs and interests. So, meetings always seemed to be calmer, and therefore more productive when Poseidon did not attend. It just was not as much fun, as Zeus really enjoyed listening to their banter.

Zeus's sister, Hera, was also a permanent member, and she was a strong advocate for improving human interests. Her desire for harmonious family units and a commitment to fidelity were common themes for her. These ideals often placed her at odds with her two brothers. She championed motherhood and birth, and was often away aiding human couples with their difficulties of conception and childbirth.

Zeus's other sister, Demeter was also a permanent member, and she always attended the meetings. Her input was also human orientated as she focused on grains and crops for humans to cultivate and harvest. She too was often away from Mount Olympus doing her divine work enriching human activities. Her contribution to the council was always solid and respected. Hera's and Demeter's permanency on the council was a condition that they insisted on for giving their support for Zeus's ascension to the role of king when they defeated their father, Cronus. His other sister, Hestia, and the other brother, Hades, were offered the same inclusion, but both had declined, despite supporting his rule.

Prometheus was also a regular member. His inclusion was not as a permanent council member, but his participation was customary, as both Hera and Demeter strongly favoured his involvement. Zeus would now have to go into damage control to account for his reasoning for Prometheus's internment, and he knew he would have to fend off his sisters' objections. There was zero chance of successfully lying about what he had done with him, as they both had their network of staff and informers, and therefore they were rarely surprised by announcements that anyone delivered during council meetings.

Zeus sat in his normal chair. Each had a favoured position at the table. Zeus had, at one time, installed a grander chair for himself to denote his importance. He only got to sit on it for one meeting, as someone removed it without comment or derision. Zeus took the loss well and without discussion.

Zeus now studied the attendees and decided it was time to begin his address. 'Poseidon gives his apologies, and he has asked that I vote in his absence.'

No one challenged him as this was his standard opening.

'As for Prometheus's absence. He defied my orders...'

'Your most unreasonable order,' Hera challenged.

'My specific order was to not allow humans to cook cow meat using fire...'

'How else were they supposed to cook it, if they do not use fire?' Hera was incensed.

'Zeus, it does seem unreasonable to allow them the freedom to eat the meat, but deny them the fire needed to cook it,' Demeter said adding her opinion.

Athena spoke up. 'I agree, but I note that that ruling has since been overturned, and all humans are now using fire to cook any meat they desire.'

Zeus relaxed slightly. Athena was always reliable in giving a practical and fair assessment of the situation.

Demeter was insistent. 'So, you used his well-intentioned actions as an excuse to incarcerate poor Prometheus. You tricked him. You put him in the position where you knew he would give humans fire to cook the flesh, knowing full well that he would be defying you. Zeus, will you please release him?'

'They have been using fire to cook other foods, so why not this one?' Hera demanded.

'I wanted humans to appreciate the cooking of the meat as a gift from the Council of Gods.' Zeus tried to explain. 'I knew it was only going to be a temporary ban when I imposed it, but Prometheus did not want to listen. He defied me, and so, he was punished. End of discussion!'

Everyone went quiet. When Zeus uttered those three words, they knew from past experience that the topic was now closed.

Zeus drew in a deep breath and continued the meeting. 'How well are the human's crops growing? Is there enough food to feed them?'

'Fine,' Demeter replied. She generally had much to say on the topic. She was still seething and was doing little to hide it.

'Are there any fights, battles, or wars between the humans that we need to discuss?' Zeus directed this question to Athena. She kept herself apprised of these events, and she intervened early to avoid escalation of the violence by using mediation. Athena was also a superior military strategist, and a fine warrior, but she was also determinedly convincing when advocating for peaceful resolutions.

'All are peaceful at present. The introduction of cows and bulls has captured their attention as there is much for humans to learn about managing these beasts and they are busily discovering their full potential.'

Zeus enjoyed hearing about human conflict. He enjoyed hearing the motivations behind human anger and about the strategies they used to fight it out. He wanted to hear the excitement of how one side prevailed. He knew he was not supposed to like hearing about humans waging war with each other, but everyone knew that he did. As there was nothing interesting to report, he simply grunted his acknowledgment that peace and harmony currently existed.

'Births, deaths, and marriages are routine,' Hera declared offering her report. She generally had much more to say about these topics.

'Good,' Zeus replied. By the brevity of their reports, he could tell that they were in a huff. Today, this suited him as he wanted it to be a brief meeting.

'We need additional members to make up our council.' Demeter recommended. 'We will need to replace Prometheus during his absence, and we really should have a minimum of seven attendees at each meeting.' Demeter was referencing Poseidon's frequent absences.

The council charter allowed for as many as twelve permanent positions. They needed seven attendees for a quorum, but with only seven votes, it had to be a unanimous vote for any resolution to be passed.

'Please prepare your suggestions of suitable candidates for us to discuss at the next meeting,' Zeus instructed. 'Maybe some fresh ideas and perspectives will improve the quality of the proposals presented.'

'I hear you are in pursuit of a new wife?' Hera challenged him before he could adjourn the meeting.

'What of it?' Zeus tried to pretend to be disinterested in his sister's inquiry.

'Any woman you take as a wife should be vetted for her suitability to be on this council as you would no doubt include her in all of our discussions regarding the humans.'

'Hera, you are making a good point,' he conceded. Zeus believed she had little regard for his successes in his love life, and she openly held him in contempt for his womanising ways. He was tempted to arrange a meeting with her to discuss the recent events in his life, and that he was planning to change and become a better man. One that wanted marriage and fidelity, but he feared her disbelief and scorn, and so he said nothing.

Hera herself was still unwed, and she was often criticised for it, given her role in dealing with others during their matrimonial disputes. In truth, she secretly loved her brother Zeus, and only despised him for his philandering habits.

'I have met a woman, but my future with her remains doubtful. Do not concern yourself with any rumours you may have heard,' Zeus stated, attempting to quell any unnecessary concerns.

'I hear that she is a human woman. You know that she has no place among the gods and goddesses. She will be overwhelmed by us,' Hera cautioned.

'She is a princess and she is very intelligent and adaptable. Besides, she has already committed herself to another man. Do not concern yourselves with her.'

'But you have just named the whole continent after her,' Demeter proclaimed, revealing her knowledge of his gift to Europa. 'That is quite a significant honour.'

'I am sure that name will fade away quickly,' Zeus said dismissing the point. 'It will probably never catch on with the humans. There are far too many independent thinkers among the humans, and I doubt that they ever agree to it.'

'Still, you should have consulted with us,' Demeter persisted.

'Africa has a name, and Asia has a name. This region did not and so now, it does. Europa is as good a name as any, so if it stays as its name, at least it will be a good one. Over time it will probably have many other names, but for now this whole region north of the Mediterranean is named Europa. End of discussion.'

He then stood up indicating that it was also the end of their meeting.

***

The following day, Zeus was confronted by Hera within his own palace. As a frequent visitor she was allowed free passage throughout his household, and after asking his staff about his whereabouts, she soon walked into his private retreat.

Zeus was relaxing with a cup of wine and reading a scroll, when Hera entered his room. He was neither startled, nor surprised to see her, and he did not get up to greet her. He tried to appear indifferent to her presence.

He peeked over the scroll and was watching Hera as she poured herself some wine. She was wearing her usual flowing dress that covered her torso without revealing too much of her body's contours. Zeus always imagined she had a gorgeous body, but sadly he could not remember a time when he had actually seen it. He had sometimes thought about the two of them together as a couple. Bedding his sisters and aunts was not an issue for Zeus, as it was for other immortals. The burnt orange fabric of the dress that she wore wafted about her and the patterns were intriguing as they billowed slightly with her movement. She was a highly desirable woman and he felt aroused, and so he quickly turned away, remembering that she did not like him looking at her in that way.

She sat heavily on a couch near him and sighed. Her dress rode up slightly revealing her ankles and calves. Zeus had always believed that she had a perfect figure and beautiful legs. He looked up at her face and was surprised to see that she was smiling at him. He knew from painful experience it was a mistake to make assumptions about either of his sister's intentions when they visited him in this way. He involuntarily held his breath and chose to say nothing.

'Tell me more about Europa,' she asked conversationally.

He relaxed and resumed breathing. 'There is really not a lot to say about her. She is a princess from Libya. She is promised in marriage to Asterion, he is the King of Crete, and seems agreeable enough to go ahead with the matrimony, despite not really knowing much about the man. She is quite young, and she is exceedingly confident, without being arrogant. She seems to be reasonably well educated and intelligent. She has a good head for business. She enjoys shopping, camel riding, and picking flowers.'

'Is she pretty?' Hera asked coyly.

'Yes.'

'Does your heart pound happily when you are with her?' she asked smiling mischievously.

Zeus realised that she was now teasing him and so he refrained from comment. There was no point fuelling this fire. She obviously knew a lot more about his plans for Europa than she had let on. He found that the greatest difficulty about being the king of all the gods was that he had so little personal privacy. It seemed everyone knew everything about him all the time. He often lamented that the other gods were aware of his plans, even before he had thought of them. Hera was particularly good at doing just that. On the rare occasions that he had initiated seduction of this sister, she had anticipated him and skilfully thwarted his advances within his first moves.

'Do you want to marry her?'

'I do not think she would make a good wife,' Zeus replied. He decided to throw her off by admitting that he had thought of it, but had now dismissed the prospect.

'Is she disappointing in bed?'

'Our friendship has not evolved in that way,' Zeus answered trying to keep his responses business like.

'Zeus. You are slipping,' Hera teased.

Why was it that his brothers and sisters all enjoyed seeing him tormented by love? They should want him to be happy. 'I thought maybe I wanted to. But, as I said, she is betrothed to Asterion, and she has promised her parents that she would marry him.'

'So, she is still a virgin!' Hera exclaimed, clearly impressed.
'How would I know that?' Zeus was now disturbed by the direction this conversation was going. 'Why are you here?' he demanded.

Hera was formal in her reply. 'Demeter, Athena, and I, have decided that we will be involved in any decision making when it comes to you taking on another wife. Your past relationships have all ended in disaster, and we are now agreed that you will need our guidance in selecting a bride. Whoever you marry will play a prominent role here at Mount Olympus. We want to ensure that you select a bride from someone who is suited to the task.'

Zeus inwardly conceded that she had a point. Any woman that was not up to the task would quickly end up being overwhelmed, lonely, and miserable. Being his wife was fraught with never ending responsibility and great personal risk.

As Hera made to leave his private chamber, Zeus stood up to farewell his sister. He spoke in a conciliatory tone. 'I understand.'

Zeus spent the next few weeks mostly alone. His staff noted his reduced appetite and his increased passion for reading. They were now borrowing scrolls from other gods to satisfy their masters desire to read. They were becoming anxious, and a more than a little concerned as this was quite unlike Zeus.

***

On the agreed day of their next meeting, Zeus flew off once more to meet with Europa. He landed after confirming that her ship was anchored in the usual place and that Europa was present.

The tents were set up as before and the women were happily attending to Europa, whilst the men were busily replenishing the ships water supplies. He watched Europa looking in the direction from which he would normally enter the field. He smiled as he realised that she must have also been counting down the days to their meeting.

He was dressed in his usual merchantmen's clothes. For any human to see him in his full godly attire was a danger to any mortal. Besides, his full regalia, despite looking impressive, was uncomfortable. He strode confidently out into the field, ready to accept the fate of their unlikely relationship. He planned to capitulate gracefully. He decided to remain resolved, and that he would endure his destiny without her. He would surrender without the use of pheromones, or the use of any other trickery that would normally characterise his seductions. He wanted to be true to her, and to himself. He looked up and studied her and he involuntary gasped at her beauty. The warmth of the summer had significantly reduced the amount of clothing she wore, and she looked stunningly beautiful. Her clothing was figure hugging and translucent to allow a cooling air flow through the fabric. As she drew nearer to him, he felt the pangs of arousal. He had imagined making love with her so many times, that on seeing her he could again instantly imagine them in the throes of their passions.

'Hello Zeus, King of all the Gods,' she said stopping short of physically greeting him.

She was close enough for him to smell her and her scent was intoxicating. He hoped his physical pleasure of seeing her remained contained. 'Europa,' he acknowledged.

'I think it prudent that we conclude this conversation quickly. I have no desire to create any ill feelings that might eventuate between us. I want you to know that I am flattered that you, King of the Gods, should desire me to be your wife. But as I am already betrothed, I am sorry to disappoint you, as I have decided that I will decline your proposal.'

He had expected this result, and so he said nothing. He instinctively stared at his feet.

'I also discussed your marriage proposal with my mother, and I was surprised to learn that you are in fact my great-great-grandfather. Did you know that?'

Zeus lied, shaking his head.

'Not that that should make a difference to any relationship that is built on true love, friendship, and mutual respect.'

He nodded.

'Your brother, Poseidon, is actually my grandfather. Did you know that?'

Zeus again shook his head.

Europa came closer to Zeus and kissed his cheek. She then withdrew slightly and spoke in comforting tones. 'I can see that you are disappointed, and I understand. It is a special moment for any man when he proposes marriage. It must be even harder for you, considering your position, and the consequences of choosing a bride.'

He nodded, but still said nothing. He hoped that his face portrayed a saddened man who had missed out on the love of his life. He would not plead or beg. The decision was hers and she had made it and had now declared it. He was rejected, but he remained determined that he would concede her rejection as a true, mature, responsible, and noble King of the Gods should do so. It was just that she looked so stunning, and she smelt so good, and he now wanted to be with her so desperately. He realised that forsaking all others during this period of strange courtship with her, had been a terrible mistake. It felt like his loins were going to explode. Just being so close to her was a torment. 'I think I should leave,' he uttered quietly.

'Europa turned to the tents. 'We've prepared food and wine for us to share as a final act of friendship. Will you please stay and join me?'

He desperately wanted to join her, but not in the way she was offering. He shook his head, turned, and walked back toward the trees.

Zeus was accustomed to getting his own way. He rarely lost, and when he compromised it was generally on his terms. He did not like this feeling and wanted to run away and sulk, like a small child does when hurt. He wanted to hurl lightning bolts and thunder and destroy things. He did not turn around to farewell Europa, though he felt her gaze on his back. He had accepted her decision as gracefully as he could. He would leave her now, and in time, he would forget her because he was strong and could move on. He would find and marry a more suitable woman. Perhaps one that was already a goddess and would meet, no exceed, the demands of her future role at Mount Olympus. He would find a woman that will love him unconditionally and appreciate him in all ways. Europa was only a mortal woman, and she was now best forgotten. He decided that she was just a passing fantasy, an unrealised dream, and that soon her rejection of him would be of no importance.

When he was out of range of Europa and her group, he gave into his feelings and threw a satisfying mighty lightning bolt into the clear blue sky. The thunder it produced rattled the trees and scared birds and animals into flight. It felt good to vent, and so he hurled a second and then a third. Then he rested, and composed himself, and thought about returning home. He would find Hera and make up some story about Europa being unsuitable, and that it was his decision to reject her. That on closer inspection, he found her to be unattractive, and perhaps even a little bit ugly. That she had low self-esteem, no morals, zero prospects, and was unsuitable for him in the role of wife.

No. That was not true, and it was unfair. That was unworthy of him to think that way about her. He would explain that it did not work out. They simply were not compatible. He had no regrets and that he hoped they would remain friends. He could already hear his brother's laughter as he imagined himself explaining it to him.

If only he had not just walked away. If only he had gone with her into the tent and shared the wine and food as she had invited him too. If only he had not been so quick to run away maybe they could have been friends. Maybe that friendship could have blossomed into something physical without commitments. He had many of those kinds of relationships and he always enjoyed them, so why could he not now imagine casual sex with Europa. Perhaps he needed to explore that possibility. Perhaps, he should have stayed and truly understood this feeling.

He now realised how seriously he regretted the immature manner of his departure from her. He wanted to be with her one more time. He could disguise himself, but she would be wary of strangers and shun him. Then Zeus remembered that he could transform himself into a bull. That would be the perfect disguise and he would be able to get close to her and be endearing. He could walk up to her and listen in on her conversation and he might discover her true feelings about him. He hesitated. Why would a bull casually walk across the field and go to her without a reason? It would not. She was smart and would become suspicious. Then he had a masterful idea.

Zeus manifested many huge dark and stormy clouds. He next hurled a series of lightning bolts into the sky. Their flashes were blinding even in the daylight and the rumblings boomed and once again startled the birds and animals into flight. Zeus morphed into his magnificent white bull form and ran as if scared from the thunder and crossed the field. He headed straight for Europa as if frightened and was now seeking protection.

'Oh, the poor bull.' Zeus heard someone say. 'It was frightened of the thunder.'

He slowed to a walk and glanced about him. Europa's attendants approached Zeus in his bull form slowly and with caution. They were unsure of how the bull would respond to their calming chants. He stood still and allowed them to come nearer. One touched him and caressed his furry back. It felt marvellous. One of the attendants ran to fetch Europa. Her mistress was sad at the way her meeting with the merchant had ended, and perhaps this friendly bull would cheer her up. She half dragged the princess up to meet the bull. Zeus saw her smile and he was pleased that his plan was working. They all proceeded to pat and caress his body. Zeus felt that he was in bull paradise. He received praises about how magnificent he was, and how strong he looked. Someone even sniffed him and remarked how clean he smelt. Then Europa wrapped her arms about his neck and hugged him. The action seemed to comfort her, and he realised just how truly sad she was. He heard laughter and looked up to see an attendant holding a garland of flowers that she had just braided. Before he realised what was happening, his horns were being decorated. The women were chatting happily, fussing over Zeus the bull and he was more than willing to let them have their fun.

One of the men came over carrying a spear. 'Perhaps I should kill it?' he suggested. 'We would have fresh meat to cook and eat on our journey.'

Zeus began to tremble, and the women rushed to his defence and protection. Oh, the poor thing is scared. Please go away and take that spear with you,' Europa ordered. The man bowed and left.

'Can we keep him?' one of the attendants suggested.

'No, he belongs here,' Europa explained looking across the field in many directions. 'He must be someone's property. I would not want to ruin our reputation with the owners of this land by stealing their bull. We may never be allowed to visit here again.'

Zeus gently nuzzled her in agreement of her assessment. She laughed happily and hugged his neck once more. Zeus rested on his haunches, and she almost enveloped him in a loving embrace. He leaned toward her, and then lowered himself to the ground as if inviting her to climb on his back. She seemed to understand and slowly lifted one leg over him, holding onto one of his horns to keep herself steady.

Gently, and to everyone's delight, he carefully stood up with Europa on his back. They all squealed happily as Zeus slowly paraded about, happily carrying the princess. She relaxed and leaned forward hugging him once more. Their intimacy was intoxicating, and Zeus was feeling aroused. He hoped that his giant bull member was not swelling in response to his desires, but to his dismay, he felt it was happening. He needed cold water to reverse the erection he could now feel growing rapidly beneath him. He hoped it did not hang so low as to be easily seen, as its discovery would clearly ruin the moment. He was near the cooling ocean water, and so he rushed toward it and into the water, only intending to reduce the size of his member and then he would return to dry land. Europa was startled, but instead of jumping off the bulls back, she held tight by pressing her legs to his flanks. She held onto his horns and laughed as Zeus splashed in the water.

Europa's male escorts became concerned and fronted the beach alongside the female attendants. They were calling for him to return with Europa. Suddenly he stepped into a deep underwater trench, and they fell heavily into deeper water. Europa shrieked, and Zeus became scared for her. He morphed into his eagle form, and he felt her hold on even tighter as he lifted her out of the water and flew up and into the skies.

As he gained height, he assessed the situation. He then flew toward the beach, but the men were angry, now fearing that somehow their princess was being abducted. They were thrusting spears toward them and were threatening to launch their weapons at him. Fearing for Europa, he turned away from the beach and headed out to sea. He flew for a long time, eventually landing on one of the smaller islands of Crete. He hoped that in his god form that he could explain himself and his actions before returning her to her people.

He morphed once more into Zeus and stood naked before her. She was still dripping wet and cold and so she shivered. He wrapped his arms around her giving her warmth and comfort. 'You are a crazy man.' she whispered into his ear. Her face turned toward him, and her lips met his and they kissed with such passion that all other sounds and thoughts were eliminated. She moved slightly away from him and started to disrobe.

He kissed her briefly and started to ask, 'Are you....?'

She looked deeply into his eyes and replied smiling. 'Oh yes, I am certain of it.'

She reached down and confidently stroked his erection and then pushed him gently to the ground with her other hand on his shoulder. She swung a leg over him, presenting herself invitingly and she slid him deep inside of her. In this way they consummated their affections for each other. After both reaching three wonderful climaxes, they rested and resumed talking.

'I really enjoy sex, and I had hoped to be sharing this experience with you. I am so glad we did it,' Europa explained.

Zeus did not want to infer that she was a woman of loose morals, so he carefully chose his words. 'I gathered that I am not your first.'

She laughed. 'I will not say that I have had many lovers, but the ones that I have had were all good, kind, and thoughtful men. They taught me the pleasures of sex and the modesty of being discreet.'

'I am grateful to them,' Zeus concluded. He had really enjoyed copulating with this woman.

'This does not alter my decision. I still will not marry you oh king of the gods. I will marry Asterion and bear him many children.'

'About that...' Zeus started to explain, but paused.

'About what?' she asked, becoming confused.

'My seed is fertile, and so you may already be with child,' he explained apologetically.

'What!' she was alarmed.

Zeus thought to apologise, but said nothing.

Europa visibly relaxed. 'It is going to be difficult convincing Asterion, that I am a virgin, if I already have a baby in my belly,' she conceded.

Zeus nodded that he agreed.

'What should I do?' she asked sounding concerned.

'I suggest you tell him the truth. Explain that you were tricked by me into doing it. In my experience, he will concede that you had little or no choice but to copulate with me. I have that reputation and he will believe you. I expect he will still want to marry you, and that he will welcome your baby as his own. He too has a reputation and position to maintain within his kingdom. He will want to protect that. He needs the continuity of power that comes from staying credible with his subjects. He will want the people to believe that he is in control.

She stared at him blankly.

'Do not tell him you had me three times, and do not tell him how much you wanted it, or that you enjoyed it, as too much information at this point would be a bad thing. But please do not tell him you were raped, or dishonoured in anyway, as he may feel he needs to embark on some fool hardy retribution against me. He will already know that I will easily defeat him, so do not put him in unnecessary danger.'

She nodded twice and then looked away, staring at the waves crashing onto the beach. She did not want him to see that she was now crying.

'I know it sounds like a fine line between his acceptance and his rejection, but I know you can manage it.

'When will I know if I am pregnant?' she asked now becoming re-solved to her situation.

Zeus rested is hand on her belly and then looked up at her in surprise. 'Triplets.' he announced, hoping the news would not frighten her too much.

'Three babies from three climaxes. You do have powerful seed,' she uttered calmly as if she was not surprised.

Zeus deliberated and then concluded to himself. Whether it is one baby, or three babies, it'll really make no difference now. Their deed was done.

'I will fly you as close to Asterion's palace as I can, without us being seen. Explain your departure by my use of trickery and you will be okay.'

She did not look as if she would be okay, as her face only betrayed anguish. 'Will I ever see you again?'

'I will visit you when you have given birth to the babies. I do care about you Europa. I think I would have become a better man, if you had agreed to marry me. I understand your decision, but I am also pleased we had the opportunity to consummate our feelings for each other. I will always watch out over you and the children, and I will ensure your safety and prosperity.'

She believed he meant it. She smiled and kissed him before dressing. When she was ready, he morphed into his eagle form, and she climbed onto his back. He carried her to meet with Asterion, so she could start the next phase of her life.

***

In the months that followed, Zeus had the unexpected opportunity to marry Hera. Only a small deception on his part was needed to reveal that she had secretly always wanted him. She remained hopeful that by being married, that she could turn Zeus into a faithful husband. They were married at Mount Olympus and their wedding was much celebrated. They were believed by all gods and goddesses to be the perfect couple for maintaining the prosperity that they all enjoyed. They eventually had four children together, and they lived as a family in his palace high up on Mount Olympus.

Zeus, however, did not remain faithful to Hera for very long, but fortunately for the Greek Gods and all their worshipers, their marriage did.

***

Just as Zeus had predicted, Asterion accepted Europa's version of events. They were hastily married with her family in attendance. She learned from her father that her three brothers had searched for her after her kidnap. No one had ever imagined that she would already be on Crete. They acknowledged that she was impatient to be with her future husband and were all pleased that she was already with his child. Her wedding with Asterion was a fabulous event and she quickly grew to love him as much as he loved her.

Zeus did visit her after the birth of his three children with Europa. He disguised himself as a servant and was able to meet with her in her bedchamber soon after they were born.

'Hello, Europa,' Zeus said when he made his arrival known to her.

Europa was pleased to see him and rushed into his arms. 'Zeus! I am so glad you came. Come see what we made.' She dragged him to the basinets that held three baby boys.

'We've named them Minos, Rhadamanthys, and Sarpedon,' she told him.

'Does Asterion love you?' Zeus asked as he was concerned for her. He then pointed toward the babies. 'And does he love the boys?'

'Yes!' she answered happily. 'And I have grown to love him also. We are a good match, and I am very happy. He truly loves the boys, and he wants to raise them as his very own sons.' She snuggled into Zeus's arms. 'You were so right about Asterion. He accepted my story just as you said he would.' She then broke free from him but still held his hand. 'Will you visit with us often? Will you see our boys grow up to become men?' She looked at him expectantly.

'I will visit on occasion. We should be careful not to shift Asterion's affections away from you and the boys. My presence may cause him to do so. He has male pride, and we need to protect that.'

Europa regarded him with a resigned, but totally understanding expression. She then smiled and nodded her agreement.

'I will watch out over you, and I will see that you all live out long, safe, happy, and prosperous lives,' Zeus promised.

'I hear that you are also married now?' she queried coyly.

'I am now married to Hera. We enjoy a captivating marriage. She has plans to tame me, and so my plans are to enjoy being entertained by her efforts. She is expecting our first child soon, so that'll be interesting.'

'Are you not excited?' she queried. Babies were now her life.

'Babies with godly powers can present many challenges,' Zeus explained with a waning smile. 'And this will be my first time as a father and being involved with it being raised.'

'You need to be involved. Your child will reflect your own behaviours and values. The more time you spend on their growth and development, the more they will come to be the same as you.'

'Ouch!' Zeus winced. 'I should do them all a favour, and abandon Hera before the damage to the child is done,' Zeus joked.

'Do you plan to have more?'

'Hera does.'

'I am sure I will get to hear all about it. The talk about you and the other gods and goddesses are hot topics, even here on Crete.'

'Our privacy is a luxury we rarely enjoy,' Zeus sighed.

They both stood in silence for a while before Zeus cleared his throat. 'I have to go.'

'I know.' She kissed his cheek goodbye.

Zeus morphed once more into his eagle form, hopped up onto the window opening, jumped spreading his enormous wings and flew away.

***

Over the years, Zeus kept his promise to watch over Europa and her family. He was pleased to learn that her marriage to Asterion remained happy and successful. Europa soon gave birth to a beautiful baby girl, and she and Asterion were delighted and totally doting parents.

Zeus kept his promise and visited Europa infrequently. Each time he met with her he presented her with a gift. The first was a beautiful metal necklace. Then he gave her a bronzed warrior to always protect her. Later he gave her a javelin that always hit its target. The most remarkable gift that he gave her was a mature hunting dog, named Laelaps. The dog had an endearing and magical loving quality, and with his charming personality, he was quickly welcomed by Europa and her family. Laelaps renowned skill was that he always caught his prey, and that he only hunted when he was specifically ordered to do so.

Many years later, when Asterion finally died from old age, Europa reluctantly married Cephalus. He was a Prince from Phocis, a region in central Greece. Sadly, they had a stormy and mostly unhappy marriage. Cephalus was constantly jealous of her former happiness during her marriage to Asterion. He became indignant when she had spoken of her prior relationship with Zeus, and her fondness for him. Europa had mistakenly hoped that by using her own examples of true love, that she would inspire him to improve his behaviour toward her. However, her efforts had only caused him outrage, and bitterness toward her. Sadly, for both of them, he had concluded that he would never be good enough for her.

***

In another region, the people of Thebes were being punished by Dionysus for an insult they had made against him. He had sent them a savage and magical gigantic fox, that became known as the Teumessian Fox, with commands to torment and terrorise the people with his retribution. The fox was gifted with the power to never be caught.

As it was known that Laelaps always caught his prey, the people of Thebes believed he would be victorious over the fox, and so Cephalus was contacted. He agreed to bring Laelaps to Thebes to hunt and kill the nuisance fox in exchange for an enormous fee. The resulting paradox resulted in devastating consequences. Their perpetual chase caused so much damage and harm to the people of Thebes and especially to their property, that Zeus himself had to intercede. As soon as he spotted them, he turned both the dog and the fox into stone.

Later, Zeus placed the image of Laelaps into the stars as the constellation "Greater Dog" which was later to be known as "Canis Major". He also placed the image of the Teumessian Fox into the stars as the constellation "Lesser Dog" which later came to be known as "Canis Minor." In this way they served as a reminder to all the gods and goddesses of the consequences of creating unresolvable conflicts.

Cephalus returned home and announced the death of Laelaps. The news angered Europa and during their ensuing argument, Cephalus accused Europa of infidelity, even though he knew it was not true.

Cephalus managed to manipulate her anger away from the death of her dog into doubt, and she found herself having to defend the truth of her true love for him. She eventually capitulated and submitted in acquiescence. They embraced with her promising to always be true to him, and that she would work harder toward improving their relationship.

The next day, armed with the javelin, Cephalus suddenly decided to go hunting. Europa became suspicious that he was seeing another woman, so she followed him. In her concern, she spied on Cephalus through the bushes. He heard her and fearing a predator, he aimed and threw the javelin that never missed, striking Europa and piercing her heart, killing her instantly. In his guilt, Cephalus threw himself off a cliff to his own death onto the jagged rocks below.

Europa's children, already disillusioned with their mother's tempestuous second marriage, buried her without honours, in a modest and secretive private ceremony. They grieved briefly, but quickly moved on.

***

Of Europa's three sons from Zeus, it was Minos who grew up to be the most responsible. He inherited the crown from Asterion after his passing. His two other brothers left and lorded over their own cities on Crete. As king of Crete, Minos came into much prominence when he defied Poseidon by refusing to sacrifice a gifted bull in Poseidon's honour, preferring to keep it as a stud bull. In Poseidon's anger, he revenged the insult by having Minos' wife, Pasiphaë; fall deeply and romantically in love with the bull. In her madness she consummated her love with the beast, and she later gave birth to a half man, half bull which she named the Minotaur. This crazed hybrid could not be nurtured, tamed, or defeated, so Minos ordered the construction of a labyrinth as a prison for the murderous monster. Minos regularly sent doomed prisoners into the labyrinth to meet death by the monsters' hands. The Minotaur was later defeated by Theseus, a Greek champion who was aided by Minos' own daughter, Ariadne who also planned his successful exit from the labyrinth when he was finished. She later married Dionysus.

***

Zeus occasionally lamented his unrequited love of Europa. He also remained immensely proud of the bull form that he used during his courtship of her, so one day he decided he would honour that bull as a symbol of what his love for Europa truly meant. He raised his hands to the night sky and claimed, 'I, Zeus, King of all the Gods, cast the image of this bull into the heavens to commemorate true love.'

And so, it was then that the constellation of "The Bull" that we know as "Taurus", entered the night sky.

'What are you doing?' a familiar voice challenged. Zeus turned to see his wife looking angrily at him.

'Err, honouring bulls,' he explained, pointing to the night sky.

'Why?'

'They represent a great leap forward in our diet…'

'More likely you are honouring your tryst with Europa,' Hera challenged.

Zeus remembered his own counsel to never lie to a woman, as the consequences of the lie was worse than the topic of the lie. He decided to change the subject instead. 'Do you see that cluster of stars?' I made you a gift by honouring the dragon that guards your favourite garden,' he said pointing to another new constellation of "The Dragon" or "Draco".

Hera examined the night sky and then gasped. 'I can see it!' She was clearly excited. 'Thank you, my darling.' And then she kissed him with an above average amount of enthusiasm.

He felt she meant it. Darling was a term of endearment that she rarely used. It had value, and it often resulted in pleasurable consequences. 'And can you see that tiny cluster of stars within it? They are in honour of the Hesperides who tend to your garden.'

Hera was pleased that he did not actually try to lie. Perhaps there was hope for him yet. She adored her gift and she decided that she would visit her actual garden soon.

***

To this day, there are many monuments erected to the woman whose name is still used as the name of a continent by its people. One of the most impressive is the Statue of Europa by Agios Nikolaos on the island of Crete. Another is situated at the Albert Memorial in London, in the United Kingdom.

***

Novella one - the constellation Pisces

The Greek Constellation series of novellas by Stephan De Jonghe.

The ancient Greeks identified and named Forty-Eight out of the Eighty-Eight recognised constellations. They were catalogued by a Greek astronomer Claudius Ptolemy in his publication the Almagest around 150 CE. The origins of the mythological stories that identified the constellations predate this documentation by as much as a thousand years.

Novella one - the constellation Pisces and the story of Aphrodite and Eros, the Two Fishes.

Aphrodite is well known as the Greek goddess of love, romance, and sexuality. Aphrodite is also known to us as Venus, and the planet is named after her in her honour. This is the story of how Aphrodite came to be. Born in the ocean during a struggle between father and son, she was raised on an island. As an adult she was carried by Zeus to Mount Olympus to work and play with the gods and goddesses who resided there.

After a brief marriage to Hephaestus, she formed a steamy relationship with Hephaestus's brother, Ares and they had a son they named Eros. All her life, she struggled with the unwanted, yet amorous advances of the Titan monster named, Typhon. Eventually, she and Eros had to flee Mount Olympus to escape his wrath, and they eventually became the constellation of the Two Fishes, known to us as Pisces.

This book is now also available

Novella two – the constellation of Capricorn

Novella two – the constellation of Capricorn and the story of Pricus the Sea-Goat.

Pricus is an old sea-goat with a problem. He is regarded as the old man of the sea. The younger generation wants desperately to abandon the old ways and leave their ocean home to live a more adventurous life on the land. The sea-goats are able to morph from sea-goats into land goats when they emerge from the surf to walk on land. They quickly learn to morph into human form, and to their delight discover that they can have much more fun exploring the plethora of opportunities that await them. In their naivety they make many mistakes, some ending in tragedy. Pricus is desperate to save the younger generation from themselves, and so must become increasingly resourceful do so, and do so in a way that his solution remains permanent. His dedication to his own kind earns him his place as the constellation of the sea-goat, known to us as Capricornus or Capricorn.

Planned launch 2026

Novella three - Saturn's moon Pandora

Novella three - Saturn's moon Pandora and the story of the first human woman.

Zeus, king of the Greek God's, commissioned his son Hephaestus to craft the first human woman. Aided by Athena, he carefully researched the perfect form and then moulded her from clay He then painted and glazed her into the perfect woman. After being fired in his kiln, she was given the breath of life by the wind god Zephyr. She was named Pandora, being the bearer of the gifts bequeathed to her by the gods and goddesses of Mount Olympus. Her main purpose for humanity was to become the role model for all future human women. Zeus then commanded that she be properly trained so that she can navigate life's complexities, but her tutors do too good a job with her, and she becomes too powerful for a normal human life. Zeus became disillusioned with her and he decided that she should be married off to a minor god, so that she'll do no harm to herself, or to others.

Pandora's story is so significant that she is honoured as Pandora, one of Saturn's moons.

This book is now available

Novella four - the constellation Taurus

Novella four - the constellation Taurus and the story of the Jupiter's moon Europa and her meeting with the white bull.

When Zeus, king and master of the gods and goddesses of Mount Olympus finds himself between wives he sets out on a desperate search for the perfect woman to marry. On a sunny field, set among spring flowers, on a stretch of land adjacent to the sea, he finds her. She is Europa, a gorgeous African princess. For Zeus, it becomes love at first sight. In his infatuation for this woman, he tries numerous times to impress her, and almost succeeds. Sadly, for Zeus, his one true love is betrothed to another, and sadly for Zeus, a daughter must do her duty. Disguised as a magnificent white bull, he tries one last desperate attempt to have her. The consequences of his quest for true love are celebrated as the constellation of the white bull, know to us as the Taurus.

Also commemorated in this story is the constellation Draco, known as Ladon the Dragon. Also featured is Laelaps as the constellation Canis Major or Greater Dog, and the Teumessian Fox as the constellation Canis Minor or Lesser Dog.

This book is now available

Novella five- the constellations Scorpio & Orion

Novella five- the constellations Scorpio & Orion and the story of the scorpion verses the hunter.

Artemis is the goddess of the forests and of the hunt. She befriends a hunter named Orion. Their friendship is slowly progressing toward a blossoming romance when Orion boasts of his ability to wantonly kill all the animals that cross his path. Artemis is dismayed. Her policy is to only kill for food, to kill for pleasure is an outrage. She feels she must sacrifice her future relationship by stopping Orion from completing his boast. She manifests a giant scorpion and sends it to attack and destroy Orion. A massive battle ensues and both are defeated, thus preserving animal life from indiscriminate killings. To celebrate the outcome and to remind us that all life is precious, their images are cast into the heavens as the constellation *Orion* and the constellation of the Scorpion known to us as *Scorpio*.

Planned launch 2025

Novella six - the constellation Aries

Novella six - the constellation Aries and the story of Chrysoma-llos the Ram.

Born from a union between Poseidon and Theophane on a remote island that was the home of a flock of sheep. They are interrupted by shepherds during copulation, so they disguised themselves as sheep to avoid the embarrassment that Theophane might suffer if their tryst became public knowledge. Their male child is born with the ability to morph from human form into a ram. From his father, he has long golden hair, and when he becomes a ram, he has golden fleece. He has wings and the ability to fly.

He is named Chrysomallos and he is raised by his loving mother Theophane. He eventually befriends princess Helle who live in a nearby kingdom. When their lives become perilous, Chrysomallos the flying, golden fleeced Ram, comes to their rescue. His bravery is celebrated as the constellation of the Ram, know to us as *Aries*.

This book is now available.

Novella seven - the constellation of Ophiuchus

Novella seven - the constellation of Ophiuchus and the story of Asclepius the serpentius or serpent bearer.

Asclepius was the son of Apollo. When Apollo had to rescue Asclepius from his dying mother's womb, he realised that he did not know enough about medicine and surgery, and so he set about discovering as much as he could. He later taught all that he learned to his son. Next, to further his education, Apollo decided that Asclepius would learn even more from the tutor Chiron. Through him he completed his training and went on to be the foremost authority on how to manage illness and repair injuries. His wife Epione and he had five daughters and three sons, and all became involved in the practice of medical treatments. The most prominent daughter was Hygieia and the practice of hygiene is named after her.

Both Apollo and Asclepius have been forever revered as the fathers of medical treatments and their names were included in the original Hippocratic Oath, that all medical practitioners swore upon when becoming formally registered to become doctors.

His dedication to healing the sick and injured was commemorated in the night sky as the constellation *Ophiuchus.* Many people who practice in astrology believe that Ophiuchus is the unrecognised thirteenth star sign.

Also featured is the constellation of *Serpens* or "The Snake," who Asclepius witnessed bringing healing herbs to another snake who was sick, and this event started him on his discovery of benefits of medicinal herbs.

Planned launch 2026

Novella eight - the constellations of Cancer & Leo

Novella eight - the constellations of Cancer & Leo and the stories of Karkinos the giant crab, Zosma the Nemean lioness, Astron the hydra, Aquila the eagle, Sagitta the arrow, and the constellation named after Herakles the Demi-God.

The birth of Herakles was surrounded by controversy. Being the demi-god son of the King of all the gods, he found it difficult to live a routine life with his wife and children.

Herakles was persecuted by Hera for being her husband Zeus's illegitimate son, and so he was inflicted by incessant painful headaches. He was told of a remedy by the oracle in Delphi, but before he could be cured, it required him to agree to take on many incredible tasks which were assigned to him by the local king. By completing these labours, he should be able to go on to live a long and fulfilling life.

He later became immortal, and Herakles is forever remembered as a Greek Mythological hero for defeating the giant crab that became known as constellation Cancer. He also killed the man-eating lioness that became known as the constellation Leo. He slew the serpent of Lake Lerna, which is now known as the constellation Hydra.

Herakles used an arrow now known as the constellation Sagitta to kill a giant eagle that became to be known as the constellation Aquila or "The Eagle".

Herakles was finally accepted at Mount Olympus and was honoured with the constellation Herakles also known as Hercules.

This book is now available

Novella nine - the constellation Gemini

Novella nine - the constellation Gemini and the story of the twins, Castor and Polydeuces.

Leucippe was desperate to become a grandmother. Fed up with her son-in-law's lack of progress, she asked Zeus for help. When Zeus arrived, he took the opportunity, disguised himself as a swan, and then he did much more than just arrange for Leda to become pregnant.

The Spartan twins grew up to become skilled horsemen, hunters, warriors, and adventurers. They embarked on many journeys together and their adventures included sailing on the Argo with Jason on his quest for the golden fleece, being hunters at the Calydonian wild boar hunt, and fighting Trojans at Troy. It was their sister Helen, who was the central reason for that protracted war.

The twins were honoured by Zeus for their bravery and commitment to each other, and he cast their image into the night sky to be forever remembered as the constellation of the Twins, which is now known as *Gemini*. Also featured in this story is the constellation The Swan or *Cygnus*.

This book is now available

Novella ten - the constellations of Virgo & Libra

Novella ten - the constellations of Virgo & Libra and the story of the Astraea the maiden, and Themis the scales.

Astraea and Themis were both goddesses who were committed to advancing the living conditions of the humans who lived on the island of Thera. Along with other gods and goddess they believed that they'd become the role models for all future human progress advancements.

Astraea strongly believed in justice and sort punishment for those that transgressed against the common good. Her belief was that punishment was a deterrent and that the formal process of trial and conviction for those found guilty of a crime had a place in society.

Themis was more about bringing about restitution to an aggrieved person who was treated unfairly by another. He mediation skills gave rise to the belief that there was always a remedy when agreements fell apart.

However, the speed of their progress and their intentions to achieve self-determination worried Zeus. After inspecting the work and assessing all that had been achieved, he concluded that it must come to an abrupt end. And as every Greek immortal knows, when

Zeus is determined and has made up his mind, nothing stops it his decision from happening. For Astraea the decision was devastating, so she cast herself into the night sky as "the maiden", forever watching over humanity as the constellation **Virgo**.

Themis was later honoured for her balanced outlook on life and is remembered as the scales as she evenly balanced out her reasoning and decisions. She is now known to us as the constellation **Libra**.

Planned launch 2025

Novella eleven – the constellation Aquarius

Novella eleven – the constellation Aquarius and the story of Ganymede the water bearer.

Ganymede was adopted by a family of shepherds when he was found abandoned as a young child. He preferred his own company, and whilst good at caring for the sheep he was regarded as a misfit by his adopted family.

One day, as he was tending the sheep, he was spotted by Zeus, who flying past in his eagle form. Out of curiosity Zeus landed to meet the young man and became quickly enamoured with him. Ganymede found himself attracted to the powerful God and very much wanted to be with him. Zeus easily convinced the young man to give up his shepherding life and come with him to Mount Olympus.

Ganymede became Zeus's friend and lover. He took over the role of cup bearer during important civil functions from Zeus's daughter Hebe, as she had found love and married a Greek Hero. Ganymede quickly became fascinated with aqueducts and fountains, and he was responsible for improving the water quality and availability of clean drinking water to Mount Olympus's inhabitants. His contribution is celebrated as the constellation of the "water bearer" now know to us as **Aquarius.**

Planned launch 2025

Novella twelve – the constellation of Sagittarius

Novella twelve – the constellation of Sagittarius and the story of the "Archer" Crotus.

A water Naiad nymph named Eupheme was a demi-goddess of the Hippocrene freshwater spring near Mount Helicon. She was youthful, very beautiful, and powerful. She met and had a relationship with the God Pan, a Satyr, famous for playing the pipes was the god of shepherds, flocks, rustic musicians, and improvisation. Their romance led to the birth of Crotus.

Crotus was a Satyr and grew up to be like his like his father, preferring the company of muses. Most Satyrs preferred the company of Dionysus, God of wine, revelry, and debauchery, so Crotus was unusual in this way.

The muses were providers of inspiration to artists, musicians, poets, story tellers, artisans, entertainers, and dancers. They brought out the natural talents of those they inspired, and positively encouraged them to excel by pursuing their passions and striving for perfection in their chosen art form.

Crotus was also a great hunter, and many say that he invented the hunting bow. He was more popular as a musician and his most noteworthy contribution to   performance music was the addition of rhythmic beats used to accompany the musician's musical score. He was also responsible for the introduction of a ritual applause to signify both pleasure from the performance and gratitude to the artist for their dedication to the composition and the quality of the performance. The applause was widely recognised as a significant motivator for artistic excellence.

Crotus was a mortal, and when he died, the Younger Muses petitioned Zeus to have his likeness immortalised as place in the night sky. Their petition was positively received, and, in his honour, he created the constellation of the Archer which is known to us as **Sagittarius**.

Planned launch 2026

Novella thirteen – the constellation Centaurus

Novella thirteen – the constellation Centaurus and the story of the tutor Cheiron.

Cheiron was a centaur who became the tutor to many of the legendary heroes of Greek mythology. Unlike other centaurs, Cheiron was intelligent, civilised and very kind. He was the teacher of students that included Jason, Castor, Polydeuces, Asclepius, Peleus, and Achilles and he taught them philosophy, archery, hunting, medicine, music, gymnastics, and the art of prophecy.

His life ended tragically when he was accidently struck with a poisoned arrow by his close friend, Herakles. Herakles had loosed the arrow in an attempt to ward off marauding cruel centaurs who came to cause mischief to Cheiron, but in the confusion, Cheiron stepped into the path of the arrow and was stuck. His immortality prevented his death, but the strong   poison caused him everlasting agony. He decided to surrender his immortality to Zeus so that he could pass into the underworld. He was then commemorated as the constellation of the Centaur and is known to us as **Centaurus.**

Planned launch 2025

The other Greek constellations that are yet to be featured include Andromeda, Ara, Auriga, Boötes, Cassiopeia, Cepheus, Corona Australis, Corona Borealis, Corvus, Crater, Delphinus, Equuleus, Eridanus, Lepus, Lupus, Lyra, Pegasus, Perseus, Piscis, Austrinus, Triangulum, Ursa Major, Ursa Minor, and Argo Navis (now divided into Carina, Puppis, and Vela)

Follicle Farm – A novel adventure

Follicle Farm – A novel adventure. (Fiction)

Follicle Farm is a comical and imaginative insight into organisational structure and behaviour of the trillions of cells that make up the microscopic world of every living person. It reveals how cells within the human body really think and how they, mostly, work well together. Bobby is a Mitochondria, and he works as a humble Follicle Farmer. He, with millions of colleagues, are part of the amazing organisation dedicated to growing hair for the human male that they live inside of. Recently, Bobby made an important discovery when he learned how to reverse the effects of alopecia and greying hair. Now it's up to management to debate if they should use his technique.

Join Bobby as he travels the body, ably assisted by Banjo and Skip, as he meets and deals with other human cells in various systems throughout the body. Bobby quickly learns there is more to management than just servicing the body's needs. Cliques, quirks, politics, unions, and hidden agendas, all thrive in Bobby's world.

You'll share in his adventure of personal growth as he encourages other Follicle Farmers to utilises best practices in growing quality hair.

This book is now available

Your concise guide to the meaning of life

Your concise guide to the meaning of life. (Non-Fiction)

This is a serious book designed to help people. Its main purpose is to assist you on how to gain insights on how to live a happier and more fulfilled life. It will give you, the reader, instant benefits. It is peppered with many great quotes, many of them are my own. I've combined my interest in philosophy, sociology, psychology, and history to delve into the true meaning of life. The reader will not only understand why they are here, but how to make their experience more meaningful.

My main aim is to inspire readers into taking more control of how they make decisions that positively affect their achievements, successes, happiness, and therefore their well-being. The book is a summary of concise points that are easy to learn and apply to the readers life for an immediate benefit. It includes popular relevant quotes to re-enforce the messages and teaching. I have also included personal anecdotes that give real life and meaningful examples of how the material applies to all readers.

Topics include
- an explanation the main purpose for living.
- how to improve your relationships.
- how communication works and how to
  make it more effective.

- understanding your needs and desires and
  how to improve outcomes for yourself.
- understanding what motivates other people.
- how to exceed your own expectations.
- understanding your own personal legal,
  moral, ethical, and value system.
- improving your control over your emotions.
- understanding the concepts of faith,
  fate and fairness.
- and being better prepared for the
  final stages of your life.

This book is now available